T0078119

Jeremy

M. Susan Thuillard

authorHOUSE®

AuthorHouse™
1663 Liberty Drive
Bloomington, IN 47403
www.authorhouse.com
Phone: 833-262-8899

Published by AuthorHouse 07/29/2021

ISBN: 978-1-6655-3354-6 (sc)
ISBN: 978-1-6655-3353-9 (e)

Print information available on the last page.

Jeremy

Ten-year old Jeremy stood by the window, looking out over the spacious lawn to the street beyond. *It was a bad dream,* he told himself. *Or, wait! I might have watched a scary movie and then had a bad dream.* He looked up the street, watching the swaying of the trees in the morning mist.

Suddenly, he saw a woman wielding a knife, or a sword, because it was big. She was stabbing someone over and over, yelling, covered in blood. Jeremy shook himself. "That was not Mom," he mumbled. "It looked like Mom, but it wasn't. Mom isn't like that." Tears coursed down his face and he wiped them away angrily. "It was a dream! It was just a dream!" He whispered fiercely. He caught sight of a yellow bus through the trees out the window. "The bus!" He called out. He grabbed his book bag and ran down the stairs, averting his eyes from the kitchen and dining area. He didn't want to see anything. The dream was still too fresh in his mind. He raced to the front door and ran to the street just as the bus came to a stop.

On board, he sat with Kelli. She didn't like him so she wouldn't talk to him. He could sit here quietly and relax. But, Bobby was behind him and reached over the seat and grabbed his ball cap. "What's wrong, Jerry? Get up late again?" Bobby laughed, throwing the cap toward the back of the bus. Jeremy didn't look back. He knew the cap would be passed around, stepped on, and he'd have to get it when they stopped at the school. He sat looking out the window. "Maybe I'll have my Mom kill you, too," he mouthed to the window. He fought the tears that threatened again. *Do not cry! Do not let them make you cry! They don't know who they're dealing with.* He closed his eyes and tried to think of anything but the images rolling around in his head. *It had to be a dream, just a bad dream.*

When the bus stopped at the school, Jeremy sat in his seat until almost everybody was off the bus. "Are you gonna move?" Kelli asked.

Jeremy forgot she was there, between him and the window. He got up and stood in the aisle while Kelli scooted past him. Then he walked to the back of the bus and hunted for his ball cap. It was crushed against the floor, torn in two places. He shook it out and put it on. Rage built up inside him and for a moment he stood with his fists clenched at his sides. The world disappeared, replaced with the red mist, again. He hated the red mist. It reminded him of blood. He became aware that he was rocking on his feet and someone was speaking.

"Jeremy, are you okay?" The bus driver and sidewalk monitor stared at him from the front of the bus. They looked so far away, small, like insects, surrounded by the red mist. *Maybe Mrs. Martin did it,* he thought. *It wasn't Mom, it was Mrs. Martin.* Almost imperceptibly, he shook his head and walked to the front of the bus. "Did they take your hat again?" The kindly bus driver, Mr. Jones, asked.

"It don't matter," he mumbled as he squeezed past them and out of the bus.

"He gets picked on all the time," he heard Mr. Jones say to Mrs. Martin. "He doesn't deserve that. If I catch them at it, I stop it, but I'm only one man." The conversation faded from his hearing.

Jeremy threw himself into school work all day. He didn't talk to anyone, just did his work and went to the library to study during lunch hour. He didn't want to play or talk to anybody. He watched the clock move forward with alarming speed. Soon it would be time to go home. He didn't want to go there. He wanted to run away and hide.

Mrs. Williams watched Jeremy in her classroom. He had never shown this kind of diligence to his work. He usually had to be prompted to work instead of playing or talking with his classmates, or some unseen somebody out the window. Not today. He looked anxious, sometimes staring out the window. She thought she caught a look of terror cross his face and wondered what was wrong. At afternoon recess, when he again didn't go outside, she sat beside him at the reading table. "What's wrong today, Jeremy? You're acting unlike your normal self. I haven't seen you smile one time."

Jeremy tried to ignore her. He liked Mrs. Williams, but she wouldn't understand his weird and crazy dreams, would she? He looked up at her, but was afraid of the compassion he saw there. He thought he might cry. He shook his head and whispered, "Nothin', just nothin'."

He paused, tracing an imaginary circle on the table with his finger. "I just had a bad dream 'cause I watched a dumb movie, I think."

"It must have been a doozy," she commented with a kind smile. "What can I do to help you?"

"I'll be okay," he mumbled into his shirt. "Don't worry."

But, Mrs. Williams did worry. That afternoon, she made notes about Jeremy's behavior. Not that it was bad, just that it was odd for a 10-year old. When he wasn't doing the assigned work, she watched him work ahead in math and read his history book. Even when one of the other children spoke to him, he didn't respond, or he just shrugged, shook his head, or waved them off.

After school, Jeremy walked to the bus with his head down. Mrs. Williams watched him walk through the halls and down the steps. He didn't respond to anything, jostling children, the custodian's jokes, or the door that hit him in the back. He stopped outside the door and stuffed his ball cap into his backpack before plodding to the bus. "That boy changed that very day," Mrs. Williams would say sometime later, when questioned about him. "He was just never the same boy again."

At home, Jeremy stood alone on the sidewalk staring up at the house. The neighbor's little Chihuahua yapped at him, creeping closer on the grass. Jeremy picked up a rock and threw it at the dog and was rewarded by a high-pitched yelp. "Too bad it didn't die," he sighed. Turning back to his house, he walked to the door and let himself in. He could smell cookies. As he passed through the hallway to the stairs, his mother called out to him.

"Is that you, Jeremy?"

"Um…yeah," he answered, one foot already on the bottom step.

"Well, come here. Don't you want a cookie? Maybe some milk?"

Jeremy put down his backpack and turned to stare at the arched doorway leading into the dining room and beyond, into the kitchen. Slowly, he stepped to the doorway and peered through the dining room and into the kitchen. His mother was dressed in a skimpy, blue sundress. Her hair was messed up and she was waving a spatula around like a fly swatter. Cookies were all over the island and the cupboard. Jeremy swallowed hard as visions of Mom wielding a bloody butcher knife flashed through his mind. He couldn't move.

"What's wrong with you?" Mom asked. "You look like you've seen a ghost or something." She smiled at him, then turned her attention to her baking.

Jeremy looked furtively for ghosts in the room, but saw none. "I've got homework," he mumbled.

"It's Friday. Why would you have homework? Come over here and get a cookie!"

Jeremy looked down at the carpet before his feet. "Can't you bring me a couple to eat in my room?"

"Since when do you eat up there?"

"Never. I thought maybe just this once…" He drew circles on the wall with his finger.

"Well, think again. Rules is rules." She laughed aloud.

Jeremy shuddered at the sound, but didn't respond.

"Okay, Kid, we need to talk," Mom said, all serious-like. "So, come in here and have a cookie with me."

Jeremy swallowed hard and sighed even harder as he began to inch toward the kitchen. With each step his heart pounded. The kitchen counter loomed bigger and bigger. Everything seemed to slow down and he suddenly noticed details – the pans hanging over the counter were swinging just a little, the clock was ticking loudly, dust on the floor looked like grains of sand, a smear of blood shone black under the chair at the desk. *It must be blood,* he thought. *What else could it be?* Jeremy stopped, unable to step onto the tile floor of the kitchen, the place where his dreams had taken place. Jack's hat laid on the desk, just like always. Jeremy stared at it, willing Jack to walk in through the garage door and get it.

Anna looked at her son impatiently. Her eyes were drawn toward the desk where he was looking. *I thought I cleaned up everything,* she thought. "It's okay," she tossed the cap into the trash can. "He won't be back. He's gone for good."

"Gone?" Jeremy's voice had become a whisper.

"What is wrong with you? Yes, he's gone. He won't ever yell at you again, or spank you, or put you into another time out."

"No more fishing?" He squeaked.

"Maybe I'll take you fishing," she answered. "Anyway, he's gone." She handed him a cookie.

Jeremy flinched as her fingers touched his hand. The cookie fell to the floor. They both watched it as if in slow motion. Jeremy leaned down and picked it up. It was still slightly warm. He held it between his hands, thinking about how cold Mom's fingers had felt.

"Do you want some milk?" Anna asked woodenly.

"Okay." Jeremy closed his eyes and walked to the table, across the room. He carefully skirted the space between the island and the table, even though he didn't look at it.

Anna put a plate of cookies between them and poured a glass of milk. She set her coffee on the table in front of her where she sat facing him.

"Life changes, Jeremy."

"I know."

"You and me, we'll be okay."

"Can we really go fishing?" He nibbled at a cookie.

"Yeah, we really can."

"Mom?"

Anna looked up.

"Do you like me?"

"I love you. You're my son."

"I know. But, do you like boys, er, men?"

"I like you."

Jeremy finished his cookie and drank down his milk in one gulp.

"Why wouldn't I like you anyway?" Mom asked.

Jeremy shrugged. "Dad went away, then Jack went away." He sighed. "Will you send me away, too?"

"You remember your dad?" Anna asked, momentary concern flashing across her face.

Jeremy nodded. "I was five, Mom. I remember." He couldn't look at her.

Anna didn't answer, just stared at him. *What do you remember,* she thought. "You were barely three."

"I remember, Mom." He paused, looking pointedly at her. "Will you send me away, too?"

5

"Of course not! But, you know, you'll grow up and maybe move away on your own someday. I hope we'll always be close, you and I." She looked pleadingly at her son, her only child. "We both went through this, Jerr. We both loved the men we loved."

Jeremy frowned at her as he got up and walked toward the stairs. Passing into the hallway, he said quietly. "There's still blood under the desk." He kept walking across the foyer, picked up his backpack, and ran up the stairs. He turned on his TV and lay across his bed. There was no more fear, no tears; just a blank stare at the floor. Something turned inside him; he felt it, but couldn't identify it. He just knew he didn't have to fear any more. "What is love, anyway?" He whispered. His young brain felt like it was on overload as pictures from his childhood reeled through his conscious thought. Continuing to whisper his thoughts, he said softly, "Maybe Dad had one of his crazy fits or something. Maybe that's why she did it." He rolled over and looked at the ceiling. "But, what did she do with Jack? She isn't talking about a funeral. Dad had a funeral. Jack's just gone. What do you do with someone who's just gone?" He imagined his mother digging a hole and putting Jack in it. "Or maybe she threw him in the river," he said thoughtfully. Tears welled in his eyes and rolled down into his hair just above his ears. He wiped at them angrily. "Why?!" He screamed silently at the ceiling. As sobs consumed him, her rolled into his pillows where he eventually fell asleep, dreaming about the many fights and the screaming he witnessed between Mom and Jack. They never hit each other or anything, just yelled and sometimes Mom ordered him to leave. Jack and Mom both cried at those times.

Anna listened as Jeremy walked away. When his door closed, she got up and looked under the desk. There indeed was a smear of something dark on the floor and some splatters on the bottom of the desk, and on the chair leg. She sat on the floor with her head in her hands. *What does that boy see? What does he think he knows? What kinds of things is he thinking?* She got some bleach wipes and rubbed the spots away. The wood was stained and wouldn't come clean, but the floor wiped up good. She cleaned up the cookie mess she'd made and put the kitchen back in order, taking time to mop the floor, again. She could never get the floor clean enough. After Charlie died, she had ordered new tile and had the end of the island counter replaced. But, she always worried that some of the blood would show up again. It was absurd, she knew, but it's what she lived with. "I hope Jeremy doesn't have the same thoughts as I do, that his dad's blood is forever etched into the kitchen floor, that somehow, it's a part of the island now." *Maybe I should have gotten rid of the island altogether, or maybe I should just have sold this house and moved to a new one.* She shuddered as she remembered her husband slitting his throat in front of her, blood spilling everywhere. She had tried to grasp the knife away from him, but he was so strong, even as he fell to the floor. As she scooted the chair back under the desk, Jeremy approached her, unnoticed.

"What's for supper?" He asked bluntly. His voice sounded like a man's voice, not the child who went up the stairs.

She spun around, clearly startled. "You scared me. It isn't supper time yet."

"I'm hungry now."

They stared at each other for several seconds. "Maybe we could go to McDonald's," she said meekly.

"I want pizza," he replied quietly.

She smiled brightly. "I'll get my coat."

Jeremy walked outside, ending up in the garage where he sat in her car, waiting.

They didn't talk on the way to the restaurant. Neither of them seemed to know what to say to the other. They ate in silence after ordering their meal. Jeremy stared out the window as he ate, the food tasting like ashes in his mouth. Anna studied her son while pretending to look at others in the restaurant. She barely touched her food, even her salad which she usually loved.

"Would you like a box?" asked the waitress.

"Yes." Jeremy replied.

"No," Anna said at the same time.

Jeremy smiled as he reached for the box. He methodically placed the leftover pizza in the box and slowly closed the lid. He smiled at his mother again as he slid out of the booth and stood.

Anna frowned at him. "Jeremy, what's wrong? Let's sit here and talk. You seem to have some ideas about things at home and we should talk."

"Didn't you say we would be fine?" His smile was plastic-looking, like he had turned into a robot. His eyes were dark and intense, and the smile, if a smile it was, never reached his eyes.

"Yes, I did. But, I feel like there's something between us and we aren't discussing it. Won't you talk to me?"

Jeremy flopped back onto the edge of the booth seat. "Why'd Jack leave his hat on the desk?"

"Jack?" She looked stunned. "This is about Jack?"

He looked at her, his eyes accusing. He nodded, not trusting his voice. *What does a boy say to a woman right now,* he thought?

"Look, Jerr, Jack and I couldn't go on like we were. It had to end. I'm sorry to have taken away your fishing partner, but…"

"Taken away?" His voice came out in a hoarse whisper. He then got up and walked toward the door. He wished it was closer to go home, he would walk. He didn't want to get into the car with her. *"I hate her!"* He whispered into the night. He stood next to the car, clutching the pizza box. *I won't cry!* He thought. *I will never cry again! I will grow up now and I will take care of everything! No woman is ever going to get rid of me! Girls shouldn't even become women! They're evil!*

They didn't talk on the way home. Mom tried, but Jeremy closed his eyes, clenching his fists in his lap, under the pizza box. Behind his closed eyelids, Jeremy fought against crying and against the red mist that signified his anger. Images of blood and a flashing knife flitted though his thoughts. He opened his eyes to watch the traffic, trying to distract his thoughts. It had begun raining, making lights distorted in the evening dusk. "What did you mean, you took him away?"

"What?" She asked, frowning as she maneuvered the wet streets. It was so hard to see in the rainy darkness.

"Jack," he said. "You took him away from me, remember?"

"It's over, Jerr He's gone for good and nothing either one of us does will ever change that. I'm sorry I didn't get rid of the hat sooner, if that's what's bothering you." She paused, but he didn't respond. "I, uh, I can't explain it all to you right now. Maybe when you're older…" her voice trailed off.

As one day melted into another, Jeremy went through the motions of a typical 10-year old. He went to school, did his homework, played half-heartedly at recess, and took walks in the woods behind their house. It was only a small copse of trees, but to a ten-year old, it was a forest of immense proportions. When the neighbor's dog sniffed around his secret space in the trees, Jeremy calmly cut its throat with a kitchen knife he kept hidden in the dirt. He then smashed its head with a rock, four or five times. Maybe it was six, he didn't know. He dug a hole to throw the dog into, covering it carefully with sticks, stones, and leaves. The little mound became a shrine of sorts, a place where he could come and pray to….*Is that you, God?* He thought. *Are you helping me when no one else will?* Jeremy dragged some bricks and pieces of wood to place over the shallow grave. He placed a candle in a hole created by blocks of cement, rocks, and bricks. Every day, Jeremy came to his shrine and meditated. He found that he could almost feel happy as spring turned into summer and he looked forward to more time in the trees. Once, he thought he heard his father's voice. "Jeremy." It said. He didn't answer. There was no one there anyway. When he found a stray cat behind the garage, he calmly smashed its skull with a baseball bat. He thought to bury it in his woods, but threw it in the garbage can instead. As he was letting it fall into the green, plastic can, he noticed it was a female. He felt a sudden sense of glee. There would be no more cats from that one. He'd taken care of that.

He calmly went to the hose on the back of the house and washed the blood off the bat. Inspecting it showed him that there was no visible evidence that anything had even happened. Jeremy began to whistle a tune. He couldn't remember the name of the song, something about the President. He whistled louder as he marched into the house. No one was home, just him. He went upstairs to his room where he used a back scratcher to retrieve his journal from under his book shelf. He wrote about the cat. 'Another female bites the dust,' he wrote. When he finished his entry, he carefully put away his journal to stand at the window, staring out at the street. Idly, he cleaned up his room, using a handkerchief to dust off the furniture. He spent several minutes working on his bed, getting all the wrinkles out of the bedspread, making sure it was smooth. Next, he lined up all of his books and model airplanes, neatly in their rows. He checked once more that his journal was safely hidden under the book shelf. Satisfied at last, he went to the hall closet for the vacuum Mom stored there. He swept not only his room, but the hallway, as well. As he was putting away the machine, he heard the garage door open. *Mom must be home,* he thought. He went to his room to wait. He knew she would find him. A shudder assailed him. *I'm not hiding. Of course, she will find me.* He sat on the floor, near the window, watching his door.

"Jeremy! Where are you?" Anna called. His bike was in the garage, so she knew he was home. "Jerr! I'm home!" No answer. She climbed up the stairs where she could see that his room door was open. As she stepped inside she saw him sitting on the floor. The room was cleaned perfectly. "Hey, Son, what're you doing?"

"Nothing."

"Your room looks great."

He looked around him. "Yeah."

"So, what do you want for supper?"

He looked up at her, eyes wide. "In the kitchen?"

Anna began to laugh, but kept it in check because he looked so solemn. "That is where the stove and food are, you know."

"Can we go out for pizza again?"

"No." She sighed, leaning against the door jamb. "I can't afford to keep eating out." She tried again. "I have some hamburgers in the freezer, and maybe some French fries. Does that sound good?"

"I don't care."

"How was it at day care today?" He was so angry with her about being at a baby sitter.

"Stupid. They play baby games. I watched TV most of the time while I was there. They wouldn't let me climb a tree. It's a perfectly good climbing tree in their yard."

"Well, I guess other kids can't climb it, so she can't allow even one boy to do it."

"It's stupid. I'm too old to be going there."

"What time did you come home?"

"I don't know; two, I guess."

She nodded. That was the agreed upon time for him to ride his bike home. She got home at 3:30, so he only had about an hour alone. "What did you do?"

Suddenly, he smiled. "Washed the baseball bat."

Anna frowned as she let out a chuckle. "Was it dirty?"

"Yep!" He nodded, seemingly pleased with himself.

"Okay," she smiled. "Then you cleaned in here, too, huh?"

"Yeah," he nodded, a small smile trying to break through on his face.

"Want to clean the rest of the house, too? You did a really good job, Son."

He shrugged. "Not really, but I guess I could."

"No, no, no! I was only joking!" She walked toward him to tousle his hair. Jeremy stood up suddenly, with his back to the wall. His eyes looked like he was ready to run. "What are you afraid of, Son? Surely not me." She reached out and put her hand on his shoulder.

"Sorry," he mumbled, averting his eyes to the floor. *Does she have a knife with her?* He wondered.

Anna watched him for a few seconds. He was rigid as a board, his right hand was clenching and unclenching. *What's going on? What has him gripped in this kind of fear? And it seems to be fear of me.* She sighed, leaning in to kiss him on the forehead. "You're not old enough to pull away yet. That's teenage stuff."

Jeremy shrugged as he stepped away. "Going to the bathroom," he said as he escaped her grasp.

"What do you want to do for your birthday?" She yelled at the closed door across the hall. When he didn't answer, she walked to the hallway and asked again. "Jerr, it's almost your birthday. What shall we do? Do you want to go to a theme park or something?"

He opened the door and stood staring at her. "Sure," he shrugged as he moved past her into his room. "That'd be okay."

"We could do something else..." she began.

"I said okay!" He snapped back.

Anna fought back tears as she made her way to the kitchen to make dinner. "We'll eat then maybe go for a walk somewhere." She sighed. "Or I could take him for a drive out in the country. He always seems to like that," she added to herself.

Worries

"How's Jeremy?" Jean Brown asked her daughter Anna. "Is he doing any better in school?"

"I don't know," Anna sighed. "The teacher conference went okay. His grades are good enough, but he isn't participating in sports or any games with the other kids. He keeps to himself during recess, although if he thinks someone is watching, he keeps himself near other boys, evidently." She sipped at her coffee. "Mrs. Williams is worried about his 'perfect' behavior, but neither one of us can put our finger on anything truly wrong."

"How about here at home?"

"He just seems angry all the time, and secretive. I don't know what to talk to him about. He even seems like he's afraid of me. It all started when Jack left. Jeremy told me there was blood under the desk. It was tomato sauce from the spaghetti we had earlier in the week. Jack always let the dog eat off his plate on the floor. I guess that's what it was from."

"Why on earth would he think it was blood?"

"I don't know." Another sigh escaped her as she contemplated her son and his moods. "I just don't know." She felt like crying, but didn't. She realized she often felt like crying when she was at home.

"You need to get him some help, maybe. You, know, some mental help." Her mother offered. "Maybe for both of you."

"Hmmm," Anna answered. "The neighbor came over and asked if we'd seen her dog. I guess she ran away or something."

"What's that got to do with anything?"

"She accused Jeremy of doing away with it because she saw him throw stones at it a few times. It was a yappy little thing and nobody liked it but her."

"Do you think he did it?"

"Did what?"

"Killed the dog."

"Jeremy? He's gentle and quiet. I can't see that happening."

"Yes; yet he talks about blood on the floor like it's cookie crumbs. And you said he acts like he's afraid of you, sometimes."

Anna looked up at her mother. "True." A deep silence fell between them.

"He's always been quiet and kept to himself, except with Jack. I think Jack and I were only together because we both love Jeremy."

"You need to tell him."

"I can't, Mom. He's too young to know the whole truth of that. I simply said that Jack is gone for good." Another pregnant pause. "It didn't help that Jack left his hat on the desk and it was such a natural thing, I never noticed it until Jeremy pointed it out."

"Well, something is wrong with Jeremy and maybe his closeness to Jack wasn't such a good thing."

"What's that supposed to mean?"

"Oh, I don't know. I'm just looking for excuses, I guess. It's easier to blame the guy who isn't here than to think something is wrong with our boy."

"Hmmm," Anna acknowledged. "He says he remembers his father."

"Charlie?"

"Well, yes, Charlie. He is his father."

"How old was he when Charlie died?"

"Barely three, but he thinks he was five."

"What could he remember?"

"I don't know. He was there, at the accident. There was so much blood."

"Anna, suicide is not an accident."

Anna looked up, tears spilling down her cheeks. "I know," she whispered. "If I don't think of it as an accident, it drives me crazy. I couldn't stop him; his blood was all over both of us."

"I remember," Jean said solemnly. "Do you think Jeremy saw you and Jack fighting and now has the two things mixed up?"

"I don't know what he saw, what he heard, or what he thinks. He is a stranger in my son's body."

"Anna, get some help, for both of you."

"Maybe." She paused, with a big sigh. "Maybe I will."

Jeremy lay on his bed, looking out the window at the gray sky. *I hate clouds,* he thought. *They make me feel tired. I hate a lot of things, but most of all I hate girls.*

"Hey, Mom's a girl, Buddy." Said the voice.

Jeremy sat upright. "Dad?" He looked around the room. "Is that you?" No one was there. He laid back on his bed and looked back out the window. Tears filled his eyes and spilled over onto the pillow. He didn't wipe them away, just stared out the window at the gathering night until sleep claimed him.

The dream seemed so real. He could never be sure it was a dream. Both Dad and Jack were there, telling him how to 'be a man'. He didn't understand most of what they told him. But, one thing he did understand… that women were not to be trusted. Women were the reason men had to be strong and take care of each other. "Girls become women," the voice said. "Mom is a woman, and you know what that means."

Jeremy woke up sometime before his alarm clock went off. He was still laying on top of his bed, his arms beneath his head. He got up and went to the bathroom. He started the shower while he went back to the bedroom for fresh clothes. Another day of school, of time to learn more and not think of other things. After he showered, he went downstairs to have some breakfast. He walked quickly past the desk in the dining room and avoided the island. Mom had left him a note again. She went to work really early. He sighed, poured himself some cereal and sat at the table to eat.

"Do you want me to go to school with you today?" The voice asked.

"No!" He spoke aloud as he looked around the kitchen. There was Dad, leaning against the refrigerator. "You, you can't go."

"I could," Jack answered. He was sitting on the counter near the sink.

14

"Get down from there! Mom wouldn't like it!"

Jack smiled at him. "Mom won't know unless you tell her."

Jeremy jumped up, spilling his cereal across the table. With a sob, he sopped up the spilled milk and threw the bowl and all in the sink, then he ran for the front door, grabbing his backpack off the stairs as he went by. It wasn't time for the bus yet, so he stood on the sidewalk, waiting. He glanced back at the house. *The house is haunted now,* he thought. He choked on a sob, willing himself not to cry. *Only babies cry. You said you would never cry again. Be a man like Dad and Jack said. Take care of things so the world can get back to normal.* He kicked at a stone and watched it skitter across the street. "What is normal?" He asked the street.

The trip to the amusement park was uneventful. They went on rides, played games, and ate too much junk food. Jeremy gave away the prizes he won to a little boy at the gate, who was leaving at the same time, but had nothing in his hands. There was a girl, too, but Jeremy ignored her.

"Don't you want your stuff, Son?" Anna asked. "It's your birthday."

"So, I decided to give away presents, today," he said almost as though he was talking to the sidewalk.

"Do you like your new shoes?" She tried again to have some kind of normal conversation with him.

He kicked at a few pebbles beneath his feet as they crossed the parking lot. "Yeah, sure," he mumbled.

"Why do you believe your son has a 'problem', as you call it?" The girl behind the desk asked Anna.

Anna was sweating profusely. "I, well, you see, it's difficult to explain." *This girl looks like she's twelve,* Anna thought. *How will she ever understand? I just want to talk to a counselor, not go through all of these questions.* She began again. "Well, he's acted strange ever since my boyfriend left."

"Yes?" She was busy typing into the computer.

"What I mean to say is, um, Sara," she got the name from the girl's nametag. "He's, that is my son, is withdrawn and angry most of the time. He used to be so sweet."

"I see. Has he been abused?"

"What!? No! Nothing like that." She was trembling now and afraid. *Why did I come here? This is just going to lead to more trouble.*

"Well, he did see his father commit suicide when he was three." Her face flamed with embarrassment.

Sara stopped typing and peered at Anna over her glasses. Her thick, honey-blonde hair fell across her shoulders. "What happened?" She asked.

"He, that is, my husband, sliced his own throat in the kitchen. Jeremy was standing in the hallway, peering through the dining room door, in full view of it all. I didn't realize he was even there at the time. I was just trying to keep Charlie, that's my husband; I was just trying to get the knife from him." She paused, trying to calm her beating heart. "He was so little. Jeremy, I mean. I didn't think he could even remember what happened. I'm not sure about what he truly saw and what he remembers, or thinks he saw. He was too young to talk about it much then and we've just never talked about it since." She looked at Sara sitting there behind the desk. "There was a lot of blood. I was in shock, but I do remember screaming for him to stop. I grabbed the knife away from him as he fell, but it was too late."

"That's a lot for a kid to take in."

"I know."

"Nightmares?"

"What?" She frowned.

"Does he have nightmares?"

"Not anymore. He used to, and he wet the bed for a while." *When was the last time that happened?* She shook her head. *I can't even remember.*

"Anything else?"

"I don't think so."

"Okay. I'm going to recommend a counselor and a visit to our doctor. Are you interested in him having skill building at home?"

"I don't think so." Anna repeated. "He keeps an ultra-clean room, does his homework without complaint. He never has been a problem at school. Except of course, he doesn't play with the other kids anymore. Kind of anti-social, I guess." She laughed nervously. After a pause, she added, "Is it important that his father had Schizophrenia?"

The girl concentrated on her computer and typed some more into the machine. "Yeah, that could be significant. Was he actually diagnosed? Did he get treatment or medication?"

"He wasn't very good at taking the meds. And he only went to counseling when he felt like he needed it. Sometimes he would have paranoia and some delusions, I think you call it. He thought either God or Lucifer talked to him most of the time."

The secretary typed some more, then looked at Anna like she just noticed she was in the same room. "Okay, let's go up front and set up your appointments, and your son's."

It's over. It's finally over and Jeremy can get some help, she thought with a smile. "Where's my son?"

"He's right there in the family room. Do you want to get him?"

"Yes, please"

As they opened the door, Jeremy looked up with a loving smile. *Now what?* Anna thought. "We're ready to go, Jerr."

"Hi, Mom!" He stood up as he put away a game he had been playing with.

This all looks so normal. Where is the sullen, angry boy that brought us to this place? Do we suddenly not need this? Is he acting for their benefit? She put on a smile. "Are you ready?"

"Yep! Let's go!" Again, there was that sweet smile like he used to use.

"Are you okay?" She whispered as they walked behind Sara down the hallway and into the lobby.

Jeremy nodded his head, seemingly happy. He slipped his hand into hers as though nothing had ever been wrong. Appointments were made for the next month. As they walked out to the car, Anna couldn't help but ask.

"Did you get to talk to someone today? Like, I mean after you went to that Family Room while I was finishing the paperwork."

"Not really, but I'm glad we're doing this, Mom." Again, he flashed her a smile.

"Well, it's worth it all if I get my sweet boy back," she gave him a smile of her own.

"I'm sorry about being a brat." He sighed as he looked out the window. *Is that good enough, Dad?*

"*Good job, Jerr. I love you, you know.*" Said the voice.

Anna looked at her son as he stared out the window. She didn't believe him. It was too much of a change, all of a sudden. *When did I start not trusting him? He's still a little boy, after all. Oh, God, please let this work. Let him heal from whatever it is that's in his head.*

As the days turned into weeks and the weeks into months, not much changed in their household. Anna went to work every weekday. Jeremy went to school. They watched TV, went for walks at the park, or went camping, on the weekends; they even went fishing. Anna was amazed at how much Jeremy knew about fishing. He taught her how to cast better and they shared high fives when she finally caught a nice, big fish.

They also attended church on Sunday, a practice she had held onto no matter what their lives held in store. They each had therapy monthly, but it seemed like they didn't need it. Still, Anna felt a distance between them from time to time that would worry her, but she figured he was a developing teen and it was normal. Jeremy often went to the park alone, or took his basketball so he could get someone to play hoops with him, or something. Sometimes they went to the mall and shopped or just hung out. He bought a metal miniature bat that he carried with him all the time. "What's that for?" She asked one morning.

"I don't know. I like it." He tossed it up into the air and caught it. "It's kind of cool, you know?"

"Fine. Don't throw the thing around like that in the house, though. You could lose control of it and break something."

Jeremy just stared at her, a stare that sent chills down her back. "God help me." She breathed. "He looks so much like his father." A chill washed over her again. "He's turning into his father." She shook her body to rid herself of the thought, but it didn't really work.

"Jerr, you don't have hallucinations or delusions or anything, do you?" She asked.

The look he gave her was detached, like his mind was truly somewhere else. *Like Charlie,* she thought with another shudder. He never answered, just looked away like she hadn't spoken at all. *Does Jeremy have…*she shook her head to clear her thoughts.

"Never mind," she whispered.

One evening, Anna watched from the upstairs window as Jeremy stood in the little copse of trees and threw his bat at the neighborhood cats. "What is he doing?" She said aloud with a frown. Still, she didn't stop him. She just watched. He didn't hit the cats, so maybe it didn't matter, anyway. Maybe he was just scaring them away from their property. *He never liked cats, just like Charlie,* she thought.

When Jeremy was in school, Anna walked out to the trees to look around. She felt guilty, like she was spying on him. She looked curiously at the rock and brick shrine, wondering what that was about. But, it didn't look sinister or like something that could be harmful, so she left it alone, and forgot all about it.

Jeremy set up a target on the back of the garage. He practiced every day with his bat, throwing it, throwing it again. He liked the sound of it, *twang, twang, twang,* as it hit the target and bounced away. By spring time, he was able to hit the bull's eye on the target every time. The target had holes in it from the bat hitting it so hard. The next time he threw it at a cat, he didn't miss. One crack from his little bat in the head brought even a full-grown cat or a rabbit down. Sometimes he had to kill it afterward, but he always, always stunned the animal he aimed at. He also became expert at slitting the throats of animals he killed. No more bashing in heads with rocks. He kept his knife sharp, liking the feel of the metal sliding along the sharpening stone he found out in the garage. His knife and his stone were kept safely in a plastic bag, hidden in a hole behind a brick in his shrine.

Eventually, he was able to kill birds, squirrels, almost everything he aimed at. It brought him such a sense of control, this batting game. Of course, Dad and Jack were always there cheering him on. It was one night when he was thirteen, that Jack mentioned they should try a bigger animal, like a big dog; see what it would do. Jeremy balked at first, "I don't want to," he whined.

"What a whiner we raised," Dad said.

Jack agreed. "Guess he's not gonna help us after all."

Jeremy whirled around to face them, but as usual, they were nowhere to be seen. "Just give me time to get used to the idea, okay?" He croaked.

"You're weird, Jeremy," said Tommy as he rode by on his bike. "I didn't say nothing to you."

Jeremy fled for the house and the comfort of his room. He made a hiding place in the back of his closet where he could be alone, completely alone. Even if Mom came into the room, she wouldn't be able to see him. He smiled at the thought that no one, not even Dad and Jack, could find him there. He looked around the cramped space as tears dripped down to his chin. "Could they?" He mumbled. "They've never been in here, I think I'm safe." He sighed contentedly as he drifted off into a cramped and troubled sleep.

As days passed into weeks, Jeremy seemed to settle into the routine of school, therapy, and life in general. Outward appearances showed a very well-adjusted boy, eager to please the adults in his life. When he entered the seventh grade, he took a sudden growth spurt, now towering over his mom at six feet. He told his counselor that he sometimes felt like his dad was watching over him, guiding him, but he admitted that he knew his dad was dead and not really there in the flesh. *But if you could see him like I see him, you would know he is very real, Stupid!* He thought.

"Did you know, Jeremy, that your father had a mental illness?" Ken, his counselor asked.

"What do you mean?" Jeremy squinted at the man. *Is this some kind of trick? Is he trying to make me look stupid or something?*

Your father had something called Schizophrenia. Did you know about that?"

Jeremy shrugged. "Maybe," he said. "So, what?"

"Well, it's a very particular type of disorder that causes people to do some things most people would think were strange or peculiar." He watched Jeremy closely. "Do you remember anything your father did that was strange?"

"Like what?" Jeremy asked, looking at his shoes.

"Well, did he talk about people he saw that you and your Mom couldn't see, or did he hear people talking when no one else was talking? Was there anything like that?"

"Yeah, I guess so. He died, you know."

"Hmmm, yes, I did know that. Did you see it happen?"

"Sort of," he began squirming in his chair, looked up at the clock on the wall. "Is it about time to go?"

Ken looked up at the clock, as well. "You could go in a few minutes, but I really want to hear your side of the story about your father."

"Why?" Jeremy looked up at Ken.

"It might be important, give me some insight into your behaviors or thought patterns, you know?"

Jeremy watched Ken for a few moments. *He is trying to get inside my head. Should I tell him what Mom did? Would he believe me?* He looked back down at his shoes. *No, that would just get Mom into trouble and Dad and I have plans.* He shook his head to clear his thoughts, wondering how much of his thinking Ken could hear or probe.

"Can we talk about it next time, or talk about something else?" He asked. "I don't remember much, anyways. I was a little kid."

"We can; what would you like to talk about?"

Jeremy wanted to tell him the truth, but knew that it wasn't a good idea. He could hear both Dad and Jack screaming at him to be quiet.

However, he liked his counselor and looked forward to the time they spent together. He talked about school, his mom, his friends (*if you only knew I make up all those friends,* he laughed to himself, *I don't even want friends.*) and his budding desire to play basketball.

"How about baseball or football?" Asked Ken, his counselor.

"Nah, I'm not interested in those," he shook his head, looking down at the floor. A picture of his miniature baseball bat swam before his eyes. *You have no idea what a ball bat is for,* he smiled.

"Want to let me in on that thought?" Ken asked, twirling a pencil on his desk.

Jeremy looked up suddenly. "What? No! I, um, I was just thinking of the little bat my mom got me a couple of years ago."

"Little bat? What do you mean?" Ken's interest was piqued.

"Now you've done it!" Dad shouted. "What's the matter with you? Are you going to tell him the truth or something?"

Jeremy shook his head and covered his eyes with the heels of his hands. After a deep breath, he said, "It's just a small bat that looks exactly like a regular one. It's heavy, too; made out of solid steel, or something!" He looked right at Ken. "I can take out a squirrel with one throw."

"You kill animals with it?"

"Yeah, well I don't have anyone to teach me to hunt with a gun, you know. Thanks to Mom, both my dads are gone. So, I can kill rabbits or squirrels or doves and stuff with the bat. It's like having a sling shot or something, you know?"

Ken looked carefully at his patient. "Have you used it for anything else?" He asked quietly.

Jeremy hung his head. "Yeah," he lied. "I tripped a little kid with it once."

Ken nodded in thought. "Well, our time's about up today, Jeremy. Anything else you'd like to say?"

"Nope, see ya in a couple weeks!" He jumped up and reached for the door.

"Jeremy," Ken said. "Talk to your mom. Tell her how you feel."

"Yeah, sure," Jeremy answered as he fled out into the hallway and headed for the exit.

One day, in the garage, Jeremy found the old basketball his step-father had given him. It needed pumped up, so he got on his bike and took it to the gas station down the street. When it was filled, he bounced it a few times, liking the feel of being able to control the ball. He went to the park to shoot a few hoops, dribbling the ball like he'd seen professionals do on TV. He lost track of time, but was brought back to reality by his mother's voice.

"Here you are!" She sighed, walking up to him from the parking area. "I couldn't find you anywhere."

"Sorry," he mumbled, chasing after the ball that had slipped from his grasp. "Just thought I'd play a little ball."

"I see," she said with a slight smile. "Jeremy, you've got to tell me when you leave the house. I was frantic." She answered. "I finally realized your bike was gone, so I've been driving around the neighborhood looking for you." She waved her arm to encompass the park. "This is not in our neighborhood, exactly."

"It's got better hoops, Mom. Sorry I didn't tell you." He lovingly fingered the ball. "I found this old ball in the garage and went to fill it. Then I just rode on down here to play for a little bit to see if it was gonna hold the air." He shrugged.

She chuckled at him. "Okay, Son. Hey, is that Jack's old basketball?"

"Yeah," he mumbled. *You want to explain why he left this, too?* He thought, looking at her accusingly. *You want to tell me what you did to him, where you put him?*

"What's wrong with the new one I got you?"

"I like this one."

"All right." She hesitated. "Well, it's time to come home. Supper is getting cold." She began walking toward her car. "I made tacos!" She turned around, walking backwards for a few steps, then turned to get into her car.

Jeremy dribbled the ball a few times as she walked away. "I'll be right home, Mom."

That summer began a new era in Jeremy's life. He spent hours and hours playing basketball at the park. He struck up a friendship with another boy, Roger, who also liked to play. They played every day, challenging each other to greater and greater feats, in their sight.

Jeremy found that his expertise with the ball also enhanced his expertise with the bat. He could actually hit a flying, live bat and kill it with one throw. He talked to Mom about the bats and told her he was "ridding the neighborhood of the pests." She seemed pleased. He felt brave enough to bring home squirrels and rabbits to eat. Mom helped him skin them and he learned how to eviscerate them, getting them ready to cook. Mom also showed him how to make 'lucky' rabbit's feet which he could trade at school for baseball cards. His collection was growing, so Mom got him a book to keep them in. Life seemed so normal.

But, for Jeremy, life was anything but normal, and nighttime was the worst. He fought off sleep as long as possible because of the red mist and the nightmares. As he lay one night, thinking of his batting practice, he realized that his mom knew an awful lot about gutting animals and disposing of their innards. "Where did she learn to do that? Did she start out by killing little animals, too?" He pondered his mother's killing talents until sleep finally overcame him; mist, dreams, and all.

As he began high school, Jeremy joined the basketball team. He excelled in his school subjects. Anna felt that life had finally gotten better. Jeremy only had one friend, but he seemed friendly enough with his teammates. Her only doubts now had to do with Jeremy's counselor, Ken, who kept telling her that there was "something deeper" going on with him. "He's got a hidden agenda that I've never broken through to," Ken explained to her. "I'm sure it has something to do with his father and/or his step-father."

"I know," Anna admitted. "He began being secretive after Jack left. We've never really talked about it, but I think he believes Jack is dead. I believe he has Jack's leaving confused with his father committing suicide when he was three."

"Why?"

"I'm not sure. We've never really talked about it." She looked down, feeling guilty. "I could never tell him the truth, so I just let him believe whatever he believes." She looked up. "Is that wrong?"

"It depends on what he believes and how far it deviates from the truth." Thoughtfully, he continued. "What is the truth?"

Anna sighed deeply. "Jack left us because he wanted to pursue a gay lifestyle, a sex change operation, the whole thing. I didn't know how to explain that to a 10-year old, so I just told him that Jack was gone."

"Does he think you had something to do with the death of his father?"

"Yes," she choked on a sob, barely able to get the word out. She cleared her throat and blew her nose on tissues from a box on the desk. "Yes, he was barely three when his father slit his own throat in the kitchen. I tried to get the knife from Charlie, but I was too late. I didn't know until later that Jeremy was standing in the dining room and saw the struggle and the blood, the whole thing." She paused to collect herself. "Then, right after Jack left, Jeremy so much as accused me of getting rid of both of the men in his life." She shook her head as the memories flooded back. "Jack left most of his 'guy things' at the house. I thought I had put them all away or thrown them out, but Jeremy found a couple of things I missed. Last summer he found Jack's basketball in the garage. He loves that old ball."

"He says he kills small animals with a bat?"

"What? Well, yes, but just things we can eat, you know. I taught him to clean the squirrels and rabbits. It's as harmless as fishing," she paused, looking intently at the counselor. "Isn't it?"

"Perhaps," he conceded. "Anything else he's killing? Is he hurting other people?"

"No," she began. "Well, yes he kills bats, but that's okay by me." She shuddered. "I can't stand the things." She sat thoughtfully for a full minute. "He hit a little kid with it one day, I think, but he showed proper remorse. He told me all about it." After a moment, she added, "oh yeah, he has killed a couple of the neighborhood cats, you know; strays that nobody wants around anyway. His dad never liked cats hanging around the house, thought they brought diseases or something...." Her voice trailed off.

Ken sighed. "Okay, well maybe he really has turned this corner." He tapped his pencil on the desk. "I can't help thinking there's something he's not divulging."

Anna sat quietly. *What is this man thinking of my boy?* "Is there something I should know, something I should be doing?" She asked.

Ken shook his head, seemingly deep in thought. Finally, he looked up at her as he stopped drumming with the pencil. "No," he sighed. "But, I think therapy should continue. I know he feels he's done with me, but I would like to go on for another three months, at least. Is that all right with you?"

"As long as you're not witch hunting," Anna replied.

He laughed. "I can assure you I'm not doing that."

When Jeremy turned sixteen, he was involved in a tragedy. At Roger's birthday party, his twelve-year old sister fell into the pool, striking her head on the concrete side. Jeremy was the only one still outside with her at the time of the accident. He calmly told police and the family that she had tripped and fallen. He was too far away from her to help. The family accepted the accident, but Roger and Jeremy were never close friends again. Roger seemed to pull away and Jeremy was content to allow that to happen. He had been growing slowly more uncomfortable at having the responsibility of a friend, someone he might actually talk to.

After the funeral, Jeremy sat out in his little copse of trees, thinking about the events of the previous few days. He had watched calmly as Dad tripped the girl and given her a little shove into the pool. Jeremy remembered staring down at her, watching the blood spread out into the water. She never fought or anything, just laid there in the water, dead.

"She was just a kid," Jeremy stated.

"She was a girl kid," Dad said. "It's them or us. You can't be choosey."

"Hmmm," Jeremy conceded.

"She was whiney," Dad said now. "Nobody will really miss her."

"I suppose," mumbled Jeremy, his head down on his knees as he sat on the little log among the trees. "Just like the cats. Nobody ever misses them, either."

"That's right," Jack added. "You'll see one of these days."

"Who are you talking to?" Roger asked as he walked toward Jeremy.

Jeremy spun around, startled by Roger's appearance. "Uh, nobody!" He said too quickly. "Just myself." He peered at his friend. "What are you doing here?"

"I don't know," Roger shrugged. "I guess I just need to ask you something." Roger stepped up close, and Jeremy thought he might sit on the log with him, but he just stood there, staring at the little rock shrine. "Um, well, did Lily really fall into the pool?" He blurted out.

"You saw her there," Jeremy answered.

"Yeah, I know." He moved the toe of his shoe around in the dirt. "But, you didn't call out for help. You were just there, staring at her when I came out to get you."

Jeremy shook his head, looking back at the little shrine he had built so long ago. "I, uh, guess I was in shock, you know? Reminded me of my dad and stuff. There was blood, you know."

"Oh."

Jeremy willed Roger to leave, but he felt him still standing there beside him.

"I just wondered," Roger said as he turned around, slowly walking away.

"Good job, Kiddo!" Dad said.

"Yeah," Jeremy whispered as tears fell down his cheeks. "I've become a real good liar for you guys." He stood abruptly and ran for the house, suddenly feeling like a little boy once again. In his room, he grabbed the pillow off his bed and huddled in the corner near the window. Somehow, he fell asleep, only to dream of being on a long hunt with Dad and Jack; a hunt like he'd never before known, through the red mist....

Jack / Jackie

Jeremy rode his bicycle through town, aimlessly turning on streets he didn't know. *Thirty thousand sounds like a big number,* he thought. *But, when you're talking about people, it isn't that much. This is a small town.* As he passed a convenience store on the western side of the city, he saw a jeep he recognized. "Hey, that looks like Jack's old Jeep," he muttered, coming to a stop a half-block away. He watched in confused amazement as Jack, or rather a woman who looked like Jack, with long hair and a dress, came out of the store and hopped up into the Jeep. "Just like Jack did." Jeremy stared as the vehicle turned toward him, moving slowly by. They looked right into one another's eyes, recognition registering. "It is Jack," Jeremy mumbled. "But…." Jeremy frowned as the car sped away, out of town. He was stunned, couldn't move, felt like his feet were glued to the pavement, his hands glued to the handlebars.

For a while, Jeremy walked his bicycle around block after block, then rode it out of town, following the route the jeep had taken. From there, he rode first one county road, then another. He didn't care where he went. *How could Jack look like a woman? No, it wasn't Jack. Was it? Did Jack have a sister? But, it looked so much like him. He or She looked right at me.* The questions swirled around in his brain. He passed by an Amish school where children were playing on the playground equipment. He stopped to watch for a while as he slowly began to notice the scenes around him. People were walking down the road. One man rode a bicycle. A herd of cows moved along the fence munching nosily on the grass right beside him. There was a family in a buggy pulled by a black horse. They were laughing. "Why are they laughing at us?" Dad asked.

27

"Did you know about Jack?" Jeremy asked accusingly.

"Know what?" Jack asked from behind him.

Jeremy felt a jolt of fear, then pure relief. "So, it's not you? You're not a woman?"

Dad and Jack snickered together. "That's crazy, Jerr. You can see him right here!"

"I think he's acting crazy. Maybe he's ready," Jack offered.

"Shut up," Dad said.

Jeremy was startled when the buggy pulled up beside him and stopped. "Are you okay?" A bearded man asked.

Jeremy shook himself before answering, not trusting his voice. "Yeah, I'm just fine," he said.

"Are you lost?" The overweight lady asked.

Jeremy ignored her and the two girls sitting in the back of the buggy with two or three little boys. "Nah," he answered. "I'm just looking around." He got on his bicycle, pedalling back toward town. He looked back one time and frowned at the two teen-aged girls who were waving at him from the buggy. Jeremy pedaled hard and fast, trying to ignore the thoughts swirling through his brain. *Jack's dead, Jack's dead, Jack's dead,* he repeated all the way home.

Anna answered the phone on the third ring. "Hello?" She said to the unfamiliar number on her cell.

"Anna?" A slightly familiar voice said. "I saw Jeremy!"

"Who is this?" She asked.

"It's Jackie, sorry."

"What?" Anna asked, temporarily confused. "Gosh, Jack, you sound so different."

"Jackie," said the female voice.

"Yeah, sorry. What do you mean you saw Jeremy? Where are you anyway?"

"I'm in town for my dad's funeral."

Panic seized Anna as the implication of this call finally sank into her mind. "How did you see him? Where? You mean today?"

"Yeah," answered Jackie. "About an hour ago at a gas station out on Elm Street."

"Did he recognize you?"

"Oh, yeah, he knew. You never told him, did you?"

"How do I tell him that, Jack…key? Why didn't you go to California like you planned?"

"I did, but like I said already, I came back for a few days cause my Dad died." Pause. "I'm leaving in the morning."

"Good!" Anna was still reeling. "Wait! What the heck was Jeremy doing over there on Elm Street? That's clear across the city!"

"How do I know? He's your kid!" Pause. "He looked pretty shocked."

"Yeah. He thinks you're dead."

"What? Why'd you tell him a thing like that?"

"No, no, I didn't. He, well, he just thinks that. It's hard to explain."

"And you've never corrected him? Geez Louise, Annie. It's been almost seven years!"

"I know. Thanks for calling," Anna said as she hung up the phone. "Oh, my gosh, what will I do now?" She wailed as she dialed her mother.

"You'll never guess who just called me."

"Who?" Mom asked.

"Jackie," she said with a snicker.

"Do I know a Jackie?" Mom asked in confusion.

"Yeah, used to be my boyfriend, Jack. Now, he's, or rather, she's Jackie."

"You're kidding! What did he, I mean she, want?"

"He just saw Jeremy over on Elm Street and thinks he recognized him. I mean her."

"Oh, no, Anna. Have you talked to Jeremy?"

"No, he isn't home yet." She sucked on her bottom lip. "Guess I've got some big explaining to do tonight."

"Want me to come over?"

"Could you?"

"Of course. This could really be major for him. He's been doing so well and now this is thrown in. I'll be there in about twenty minutes." She was about to hang up, but added, "Anna, call his counselor. You might need him."

When she arrived, they hugged. "Is he home yet?" Mom whispered.

"No," Anna said. "Help me make some burgers or something. I need to feel normal." Jean walked to the kitchen to prepare the food, while Anna lighted the grill out on the patio. "I'm so afraid," she said, standing in the doorway. "I don't even know what to say to him."

"Play it by ear, Dear," her mother answered. "Let him take the lead and give him as much or as little information as he needs."

They were eating when Jeremy came in the garage door. "Oh, Hi Grams," he said to his grandmother. "I didn't know you were here. Is that your new car out there in the driveway?"

It was so normal, so like her sweet boy, Anna was completely speechless. *This is truly not what I expected,* she thought. She watched as her mother had a perfectly normal conversation about the new car, just like nothing ever happened, just like always.

"There's burgers," she croaked.

"See that," he smiled at her as he moved into the kitchen to fix his plate. "No cookies?" He asked with his mouth full

Anna looked pleadingly at her mother who shrugged away her fears. Anna got up to clean, her answer to awkward situations, especially where Jeremy was concerned. For his part, he ate and talked with his grandmother as if nothing had ever been wrong. Anna decided that he hadn't recognized Jack after all. She had worried for nothing. This too, would all blow over.

On the following weekend, Jeremy again went out into the countryside, riding around Amish farms. He befriended a boy about his own age named Jeremiah, who invited him to join him as he fished in a creek, and soon, Jeremy began spending time on a farm, learning to work with horses, enjoying going fishing, and the family feeling he had missed from his own home. The Fry family treated him much like one of their own, laughing at the nearness of the boys' names – Jeremy and Jeremiah – teaching him their language, and insisting he dress as one of the family when he stayed with them. Jeremy found that he liked the feeling of 'man's work', outside, getting dirty. One evening, he and his friend, Jeremiah, were sitting in the loft of the barn, their legs dangling out the loft door, bare feet swinging, when there arose a commotion from the chickens. "Something's wrong," Jeremy jumped up to go see.

"Nah, it's just *Mam* getting chickens for dinner," Jeremiah said.

"What do you mean?" Jeremy cocked his head to one side, still aware of the squawking from the chicken coop.

"Probably having fried chicken for dinner."

"You mean, your mother is going to kill chickens and then cook them to eat?" Jeremy squeaked.

"Well, where do you think chicken comes from?" Jeremiah laughed.

Jeremy walked to the other side of the barn loft to another open doorway which looked down on the dooryard. There, he witnessed Mother Fry, chicken in one hand and axe in the other, walking to a chopping block near the driveway. In amazed horror, he watched as she chopped off the bird's head, then put her foot on its neck as the dying animal waved its wings in the throes of death. Sarah, Jeremiah's older sister came with two more live chickens and the process was repeated. Amelia, a younger sister, carried the dead animals, blood dripping, to the back door where they all congregated to pluck the feathers and eviscerate them. Jeremy couldn't hold it in, he vomited right there, out the barn door. He turned to his friend, who didn't seem affected by it at all before fleeing down the ladder, quickly grabbed his own jeans and tee-shirt from a peg in the barn where they hung, and ran out to his bicycle. In a blind panic, he left the farm and never returned. *All women are evil,* Dad said. *Killing comes naturally to them. They will pretend love, then they will one day kill. You know that, don't you?"*

"Yeah? Well, what about what we do? We kill too!"

"But, that's different, Jerr," Dad purred. "We're not like them. They produce little people, then they kill their partners."

Jeremy stopped peddling and stood with his bike, near the basketball hoops at the park. "Look, I kill rabbits and squirrels to eat. They killed chickens to eat…Is that any different? I mean, why did I get sick like that?" He shook his head, walking around the ball court, tapping each post of the chain link fence as he passed by.

"I don't know!" He wailed. "I just don't know!"

He ran back to his bike and peddled furiously home where he threw down the bike in the yard and hid in his closet, in the furthest corner he could squeeze into. There, he sobbed into his knees until sleep claimed him. His troubled dreams were filled with women killing children, boy children, men, and there were feathers everywhere, red feathers, white feathers, all on a background of red mist....

The Change

Jeremy sat huddled in his little woods, knees hugged to his chest. "Where've you been?" He hissed through his tears.

"You needed to learn a lesson, and now you have," Dad said out loud.

Jeremy looked up at his father as he reached out a hand to touch his arm. But, the vision disappeared before his gaze. He looked through the leaves of the trees and brush, where he saw his own mother washing her car in the driveway. She seemed so normal, so happy. He stared hard at her, trying to see the evil. Finally, she looked his way, seeming startled to see him there, looking at her.

"Want to help?" She called to him. He thought she sounded nervous, like she didn't really want his help.

He sauntered to her and accepted a soapy sponge. After a few minutes, he got up the courage to speak. "Mom, have you ever killed a chicken?"

"What?" She stopped spraying the car, and for a moment, he thought she might spray him with the hose. He suddenly longed for her to do something so fun and simple. "No," she answered. "I buy them from the grocery. Why?" She was frowning as she began spraying the car again.

"I saw someone kill chickens and wondered if you or grandma ever did that."

"I don't think your grandmother ever did anything like that either, Jerr. She was a city girl growing up."

"Oh," he mumbled. Suddenly, he felt the cold water as it hit him full force. Mom had actually sneaked up behind him and sprayed him! "Hey!" He shouted in glee. He dipped his sponge in the soapy water and threw it at her. For a few moments, they played this game until he finally put a kink in the hose and stopped the play. When Mom was off guard, he grabbed the hose to drenched her with the cold water. She squealed in delight, running to the house.

"I'll get some towels!" She called over her shoulder.

See how strong you are, Jerr? Dad hissed in his ear as he wound up the hose and turned off the water. *You could easily overcome a woman. It isn't as hard as it seems, you know?*

"This from a dead man!" Jeremy said hotly. "Boy, weren't you just strong?"

"What?" Mom asked, handing him a dry towel.

"Oh, nuthin." He said, eyes downcast.

"It doesn't take strength to get beat in a water fight, Son," she said gently. "It was just fun, right?"

"Yeah, Mom," he smiled weakly at her. "It was a lot of fun."

They silently dried the car. "Did you really see someone kill a chicken?" She asked quietly.

"Yeah, three of them." He answered. "It was on an Amish farm and I guess they were going to eat them for supper." He shuddered.

"At Jeremiah's, or somewhere else?"

"Yeah, at Jeremiah's. His mom and sisters killed them like they were nothing." *Like you did Dad and Jack,* he thought.

"They're animals, Son. People eat animals. We eat meat, you know. Some of it you have provided, sort of like chickens."

Jeremy suddenly had a vision of his mother cutting up a chicken for dinner. He'd seen her do that before. *What if... No,* he shook his head. *I can't think that about my mom.* He looked at her working on the car, seemingly without a care in the world. Another shudder passed over him.

"I'm going for a bike ride," he announced as he ran to get his bicycle.

"Don't be gone long!" She called.

He rode to the park, but avoided the temptation to go to the convenience store across town. He didn't want to see the woman who looked so much like Jack, again. He shuddered at the thought. "I must be going crazy," he said aloud. "I wonder if I should tell the counselor about this stuff. He'd probably lock me up, or something." He stopped his bike near the cemetery. Slowly, he pedaled up the stone driveway to the back where he laid his bike on the grass and walked to his dad's headstone. As he looked down at the lettering on the marble surface, tears dripped from his eyes, splashing in slow motion onyo the words. He stared at the small pool, half afraid to touch the stone.

"So, you came to me for once," Dad said from behind Jeremy.

"Yeah, for once…"

"What are you looking for, Son?" Dad asked comfortingly.

"I don't know; answers, I guess. I'm so mixed up. I play this game every day at school and at home; I don't know what's real and what isn't half the time."

"Do you believe in me?" Dad asked simply.

"I don't know; I mean, I guess so, but what happened, Dad? Why are you dead? Don't I deserve to know that?" He plopped to his bottom, his legs crossed beneath him. "And I am totally confused about Jack!"

"I thought we had this all worked out, Jeremy. I thought you knew what happened."

"I don't know," he shook his head, tears flying. "I thought I knew, but Mom acts so normal and everything." He bawled with abandon for a few seconds. "And how can I see you, anyways? You're dead!" He screamed. "Why don't you just leave me alone? What do you want from me?" Jeremy kicked at the stone, but it just hurt his toe, even through his shoes. "I just want life to be normal again," he whimpered, now kneeling in front of the headstone.

"Jeremy," the wind seemed to whisper his name. "Jeremy…"

He laid on the ground and closed his eyes, trying to shut out the world. He lay silently as both Dad and Jack talked to him and to each other. It was like watching a TV screen in his head. He didn't have to do anything or take part, they just ran the film and he watched. He began to see it all plainly, the way women killed and men pretended to be the ones in control. *Of course men need to take control,* he thought in amazement. *If they don't, they'll end up like fried chicken. I won't ever eat chicken again.* After a while, he got up, dusted off his pants, and walked resolutely to his bike. "This will be the last time I come here," he whispered. "The last time I cry like a baby, too."

"Are you ready now?" Dad asked.

Jeremy stopped before peddling his bike. With a nod, he answered, "Yes, I'm ready. I know what to do." A grimace crossed his face, that was supposed to resemble a smile. His eyes were dull, and his face flat and blank. "I won't let them kill anymore, Dad."

As he rode home, he let go of all feelings. It didn't matter anymore what he felt, or what anyone felt. There was a job to do and through visions, he had been called to do it. He would avenge men everywhere from evil women. He stopped suddenly and sat in the trees by the roadside. An Amish family was walking down the road toward him. He sat still as they passed, laughing at some garbled something one of them said. There were three young girls, about 10 to 12, he guessed. He reached into his bag and felt his little bat, the smoothness of the metal calming his mounting nerves. He drew the bat out of the bag to caress it lovingly while he watched them walk past him. He spotted a squirrel in a nearby tree and threw the bat unerringly at the animal. It fell dead to the ground. A chuckle escaped him, but his face remained stoic and placid, formidable, yet calm. The Amish people had stopped to watch what he'd done, the children talking excitedly about the squirrel. They waved at him as he grabbed his bike and rode away, the squirrel tucked safely into his basket.

At home, Jeremy cleaned the squirrel and offered it to his mother to cook for supper. She accepted it with a smile. "Where'd you get this?" She looked at him. A frown formed as she watched her son struggle for words. She reached out to lay a hand on his arm, but he flinched away. *Not this again,* she thought. "What's happened?"

Jeremy looked at her with those dull eyes. "Nothing happened. I brought you a gift. If you don't want it, throw it in the garbage."

"Jeremy, that's totally unfair," she protested. "I'm your mother and I worry about your well-being." She poured some milk and offered him some chocolate chip cookies.

He stared for a few seconds at the plate in her hands, imagining that her hands were turning red with blood as he watched. He looked up at her face, but saw only his mother, not the monster he expected. "I can't go on pretending, Mom. I know what I know and I know what my future holds. I'm not your little boy anymore. I'm almost seventeen." He turned to walk away, but another thought turned him back around. "I want a car as soon as I have my license." Without waiting for a reply, he ran up the stairs, three at a time.

"Are you crazy?" She called after him, not knowing the portent of her words. "I don't have that kind of money, you know."

And He Became A Man

Jeremy laughed as he thought once again of his first car, the piece of junk his mom found on the internet. She'd paid $500.00 for it and it was worth about that much. But, it got him around, to school and to his new job at the local garage, where he learned about mechanics and travel from the guys who hung around the shop. There were a lot of bikers who stopped in to get work done, and they were full of stories about travel, adventure, and women. His loathing for women grew even bigger.

Jeremy graduated with honors, including a full scholarship. For the first time, he would leave his mother's home to strike out on his own. He chose a college in Pennsylvania, away from his native Ohio. He wanted to be free of the thoughts that were pervasive in his boyhood home, but after a few weeks of newness, he found that he brought it all with him. He kept to himself most of the time, not wanting to be friends with a bunch of 'pot heads,' as he thought of the boys in his dorm. He ignored the girls, even though he often was approached and flirted with. He just wasn't interested. His goal was to earn his degree in business, and to get out. He never went to parties, disgusted by the others who came in late, drunk and high. He found it to be a waste of time and energy.

Breaks he took at home for the first year. He put up with his mother and grandmother who were always excited over holidays. He didn't take part in the festivities, spending most of his time in his room or out driving around the countryside. He often parked his car at the cemetery where he sat near the grave of his father, even in the snow.

Anna worried about her son, but not overly so. He seemed calm and quiet, but could carry on a very intelligent conversation, if he had to.

He was more likely to engage his grandmother than her, but sometimes he would indulge her passion for talking. She was proud of how well he was doing in school and often bragged to her friends about his academic achievements. She envisioned him being a Wall Street tycoon someday, making lots of money and having a great life. She realized he never talked about going out on dates, but he didn't seem like he was unhappy. She wondered if he just kept his love life away from her, or if he was more like Jack than she knew.

"Where do you go when you disappear for hours?" She asked one snow-filled Christmas day.

He looked at her with those somber eyes; eyes devoid of feeling, eyes that scared her, if she looked too long at him. *His dad looked just like that sometimes,* she thought with some fear. *Was that how he looked when he killed himself?* She shook her head. *I can't remember. I don't want to remember.*

"Why?" Jeremy broke into her thoughts with his answer.

"I just wondered if you have a girlfriend somewhere or something." She said timidly.

He snorted. "Have I ever?"

"Not that I know of. Don't you like girls, Jerr?"

"Not especially," he replied. "You, of all people, should know that about me."

"Do you hate me, then?"

He leveled his eyes on her again. "No, I don't hate you." Pause. "And I am not afraid of you, either."

"Well, that's good," she replied in a half-whisper.

He gave her a look of pure disdain, a look that made her shudder, before he got his hat and coat and walked out to brush off his car. She watched from the window as he methodically cleaned his car, shoveled the sidewalk and driveway, then got into his car and drove away. "I don't even know you," she breathed. "Where did my boy go? Who are you, this man that looks so much like his father?"

During his Junior year of college, Jeremy spent his holidays at museums or travelling. He loved antiquities and spent money on investments. Italy and France had a special appeal for him, with the ancient ruins and open lifestyle. He got a job in a brokerage firm for the summer, then transferred to real estate. This was where he excelled. He loved showing properties, and found he was adept at talking people into sales. It was exciting to make one successful sale after another. The best part? He found a home for himself, out in the Pennsylvania countryside, secluded in 10 acres of woods, off the main roads. If anyone were to come down his driveway, it would be to see him. No one else lived down the little, dusty lane.

Jeremy's mother and grandmother visited his home for Christmas break of his Senior year. "It's so quaint," Mom observed. "Out here in Pennsylvania Dutch Country."

Her mother agreed. "We should go to some of the Amish shops and get souvenirs," she added. "Pennsylvania Amish are different from Indiana ones. I think their head coverings and clothes are made different."

"You want a head covering?" Jeremy asked with a slight frown.

"Well, I don't think you can buy them. I think they make them for religious purposes or something."

Jeremy was already spinning with memories and thoughts of hats. He excused himself to flee into his bedroom while flashes of memories of Jack's baseball cap on the desk and Dad's fishing hat in the closet crossed his mind's eye. *She did this to collect their hats?* He thought with increasing horror. *I can't think about this!*

Of course you can, Dad's voice (or was it Jack?) drifted into his mind. He looked around him, but no one was there. *This makes it perfect, you know. You can kill two birds with one stone, so to speak.* Jeremy shuddered at the laughter he clearly heard. His mother and grandmother were deep in their own conversation in the next room and didn't seem to notice his absence, at all. He could clearly hear them talking and laughing only a few feet away from his bedroom.

Jack, if you are dead, then what about that woman I saw? Jeremy screamed in his mind. *She looked just like you! What are you doing to me?* Jeremy opened his closet, and was relieved to find no hats in there. He held tightly to the handles of his closet doors, eyes closed, trying to regain control of his breathing.

Don't worry about her, The Voice said. *She's gone now. All you have is me.*

"But who was she anyway?" Jeremy's voice was weak, like a little boy. It irritated him that he could still act like a child. He stared hard at his hiding place in the corner of the closet, the pillow and blanket looking so inviting.

"What are you doing, Honey?" His mother's voice grated its way into his thoughts. He felt his hands clench tighter on the doors. With effort, he turned to face her, closing the doors to his closet so she wouldn't see his special place of retreat.

"I uh, well, I thought we might go out, so I was looking to see if I wanted to change my clothes," he said weakly.

"Really? Cause, you're dressed to the nines already," she flashed him a smile.

He smiled back. At least, he hoped it was a smile. It felt more like a frown to him.

"Do you mean you want to go shopping with a couple of old ladies?" His mother snickered.

He shook his head, looking at the floor as a sick thought filled his brain. "Not really, no. But if you two want to go out, I thought I'd drive you."

"Oh, don't bother with us," Mom said, waving a hand toward him as she walked out of the room.

You can do it, The Voice said. *It's the perfect time. You can surprise her with an Amish Kapp.* Jeremy froze as The Voice permeated his mind. He pictured his little bat and how it would work. He had to admit he was curious to know if he really could do it, or not. *They don't prosecute people,* The Voice continued. Jeremy realized he couldn't distinguish who was speaking to him. Was is Dad or Jack, or was it someone else? He put a hand up and squeezed the bridge of his nose, trying to stop the thoughts, and The Voice. *Does it matter who it is?* The Voice taunted.

The Executions Begin

It was so easy. She was such a slim girl, walking along a dirt road in Lancaster County, Pennsylvania. There was no one for miles, although that was an illusion, because just over a rise to the west was the village of Bird in Hand. Jeremy stopped her to asked for directions, carefully stepping out of the car. She was shy, but still, she told him where the nearest paved road was so he could get back to town. She was sweet and looked fresh, natural, smiling shyly. He invited her to take a ride in his car, but she drew back and turned to run away. A blow to her head with his little bat, thrown from his casual position beside the car, brought her to the ground without a sound. The bat made a perfect indent in her temple, just behind her left eye.

She fit easily into the trunk of his fancy blue Malibu. He rubbed her bare feet, sighing as he stared at her. Her head rested on a plastic sheet he kept in the trunk to keep blood off the carpeting, in case there was any blood. Really, there was very little from this wound, just a few drops as he pulled the bat free of her skull. He slowly closed the trunk and got back into his car. As he pulled out onto the road, he saw a buggy coming toward him. He waved them down and asked for directions to the nearest town. They were kind, laughing at his plight of being lost in Lancaster County....

He drove aimlessly, finally finding a brushy area near a pond where there were no houses, just fields and woods. He removed the white Kapp from her head and tossed her body into the brush. He couldn't move, just stood there staring at the bushes in front of him. *There's nothing to see,* The Voice whispered. *It's time to leave. Get in the car and go.* Jeremy did as he was told. He worried all the way back to town. Each car he passed was a potential enemy, could be a police officer… He drove slowly, obeying every law he knew of.

When he got to his home, he looked closely at the plastic in his trunk. There was blood on it, so he rolled it up carefully and stuffed it into the dumpster beside his garage, to be taken out by the street next week. The dumpster was almost full, and he remembered that trash pick-up would actually be tomorrow. He would empty his house trash into it yet tonight. He sighed in relief, but still looked all around the neighboring fields as though someone might be following him or watching. He went into his kitchen and ordered pizza, turning on the TV. When the delivery was made, the knock on the door frightened him. "Who's there?" He shouted over the noise of the TV. A Bonanza movie was on, that he hadn't even been watching. He had been sitting there staring at the *Kapp*, not knowing what to do with the filmy thing.

Jeremy paid for the pizza and sent the delivery kid away. He watched him eyeing his car and became suspicious of him. "What does he think he knows?" He mumbled. *Easy, Boy.* The Voice said. *He just likes the fancy car. We're in the clear. You got rid of one of the baby-makers, that's all that counts here.* Jeremy nodded as he plopped on a stool at his bar, pizza in hand. He looked curiously at the *Kapp* he had taken, wondering why they all wore these crazy hats. "Maybe Mom will like it," he said aloud. "I'll tell her it's a souvenir I got for her while she was out shopping." He smiled at his deceit, the logical thought of it pleasing him. He laid it carefully on his desk, some pizza sauce dripping from his hand onto one of the strings. "Dang!" He said.

As he stared at it, flashes of blood under the desk in his mother's home came into his mind. He looked again at the Kapp. "Is that blood, or not?" Methodically, he reached into a drawer for a pair of scissors. He carefully cut the one string off the *Kapp*. With a shrug, he decided he could tell his mother that when you get a *Kapp*, and you're not Amish, you have to have one that's imperfect, one that has lost its string. "Like this one," he lifted it up, a kind of pride filling his mind. He smiled at the *Kapp* as he laid it gently back on the desk. He could hardly wait for his mother to come back so he could give her the gift. He thought briefly of the girl who had worn this *Kapp*. She was gone, and he was sure, no one cared. "I don't," he whispered. "I'm glad she's gone, like so many chickens she probably helped kill." A momentary frown appeared between his eyes.

"You're not having doubts, are you?" The Voice asked.

Jeremy whirled around, but no one appeared. "No!" He shouted. Then, in a whisper added, "Not now, don't bother me now."

"Just saying, it's a good start," The Voice continued as though Jeremy hadn't spoken.

Jeremy fled to his bedroom and opened the closet doors. He looked longingly at his nest in the corner. As he slid down to his knees to crawl in, he heard someone open the front door. "What now?" He muttered. He sat back against the door and took some deep breaths, letting the air out slowly through his mouth. *What have I done? What have I done?* Unbidden tears threatened to fall on his cheeks. He shook his head, and with a whimper, he crawled to the bed to pull himself up. Like a drunken sailor, he staggered to the bathroom, barely making it to the toilet to vomit. He retched until he couldn't bring up anything else.

"Jeremy, what in heaven's name?" Came Anna's voice from the doorway. "Are you sick? What's wrong, Honey?"

He recoiled at her touch on his shoulder, scooting to sit up against the tub, facing her. He wiped the spittle from his chin with some toilet tissue and shook his head. "Nothing," he said weakly. "I'm fine, just choked on something."

She reached out to feel his forehead, but he brushed her hand away. "I hope you're not coming down with something," she said with a worried frown.

Grandma was right behind her. "What's going on?"

"He's sick or choked or something."

Jeremy pushed himself up. "I'm fine. I just choked on…, I just choked." He made his way between them to the sink where he threw cold water over his head. He grabbed for a towel and buried his face in his hands, drying it off. With a deep breath, he turned toward the door and called out behind him. "Come out here. I got you something."

Anna and her mother followed him to the dining room of his quaint home. He handed the *Kapp* to his mother with a smile. "Here you go!"

She looked up at him, her mouth twisting between a smile and a frown. "How on earth did you come by this?"

"What is it?" Grandma said behind them. "Oh! Where did you buy it?" She took the *Kapp* from her daughter and turned it over and over. "It looks authentic."

"Right!" He sneered. "I grabbed it off of some Amish girl out in the country!" He swallowed at the near-truth. "Can't you just be grateful for the gift? You said you'd like one, didn't you?"

Anna looked up at him. "Well, yes, um, thank you, Son."

"Look, it only has one string," observed Grandma. "Aren't they supposed to have two?"

Jeremy sighed and swallowed again, the taste of bile still strong in his throat. "You have to buy a ruined one, or one that's torn, or something. If it was whole, some woman would be wearing it, don't you think?"

"Well, that makes some sense," Anna slipped the *Kapp* on her head. "What do you think?"

Jeremy grabbed it from her. "Don't wear that!" He hissed. "I got it for your collection of hats. I'll get you more. Just, don't wear them, okay?"

"Sure, okay," she murmured meekly. She and her mother exchanged looks.

Well, how about if we go out for Chinese tonight, before we leave?" Grandma asked.

"I'm not hungry," he answered. "You go ahead." He looked at the counter, remembering the pizza. "I bought a pizza. It's over there if you want some."

"We could order in," Anna said at the same time. "We came to spend time with you, Jerr."

Jeremy shuddered at the nickname Jack and Dad always used. He wished she wouldn't do that, but decided it was part of his punishment for the things his mother had taught him to do. "Do what you want," he said as he walked to the kitchen for a drink of water.

"Oh, look! There's pizza." His grandmother announced.

"I just said that, didn't I?"

"Did you?" She smiled sheepishly.

"We can eat pizza, Anna. Get some napkins and we'll have some together."

"I'm not hungry," he repeated.

"Jeremy, there's something wrong," Mom said, twirling the *Kapp* on her fingers.

Sweat trickled down his back. "What?" He squeaked.

"I just don't like the way you're acting. You must be getting sick if you're not eating."

"I already had some, Mom." He turned away from the two of them and sat on the sofa in the living room, propping his feet on the coffee table, and leaning back with eyes closed. "It's what I choked on. I don't want any more right now, okay?"

"You're more than ready for us to go home, aren't you?"

He paused. "I guess so. I'm used to being alone."

"Don't you have a girlfriend or someone to do things with?" Grandma inquired.

"No!" He sat up and looked fiercely at them. Blowing out a breath, he continued. "Look, I have friends, but I don't need another woman telling me what to do. I have the two of you for that." He gave them a weak smile.

Grandma snorted and Anna chortled at his remark. "Okay, okay, we get it. Go home and leave me alone!"

He shrugged as he leaned back on the sofa again.

"We'll leave in the morning, Son. Before breakfast." After this remark, they ate before Anna cleaned up the leftover food. "I love you, Son," she said as she and her mother went to the guest room.

"Me, too, Jeremy," Grandma added. "Can I have a hug?" She stood by the coffee table, waiting.

Jeremy got up and hugged them both. A shudder passed over him at his mother's touch.

"Thanks for the hat," she said sweetly.

He looked into her eyes. *Was that a smile? Does she know?* He felt his pulse quicken at the thoughts. But, the moment was gone. She waltzed off into the bedroom where she closed the door softly. *She's sleeping on my sheets,* he thought. *I'll have to wash them at least twice to get her scent off of them. Maybe, I'll just throw them in the garbage.* He pictured his sheets lying next to the bloody plastic in the land fill and shuddered. But, as he thought about that, he decided it was a type of poetic justice, a step closer to his goal. *Wait, what? What am I thinking?*

"The ultimate goal, of course, is for this to end where it began," said The Voice.

"Time for that, Son," Said Dad. "Time for that later. For now, you have begun something. Yes, you have begun something, indeed."

Missouri

It was in Missouri that Jeremy noticed the voices had stopped. He had gone to St. Louis to a specialized sales training for two weeks. Then, there was an assignment in Jamesport, a pending sale in his new profession, national realty sales. He obtained listings in various states, contacted people over the internet and by phone, and finalized the sale in person. It was great work that allowed him to travel a little bit, not too far from home, but far enough to feel he was accomplishing something beyond what others had done.

He came upon the girl by accident. He had been looking for a remote campground for his RV and had been directed to a place on the outskirts of Jamesport. There, he encountered Amish, again. He drove quickly past a small community and right into the park. When he registered his site, he realized the girl behind the counter was clearly Amish. One of the first things to catch his eye was the *Kapp* on her head. *Mom was right,* he thought. *the stupid little hats are different here.*

"You'll have to get her one of these," The Voice entering his mind shocked him, causing him to drop the pen he'd been using. He shook his head to clear his thoughts.

"Do you live around here someplace?" He asked with what he hoped was a look of innocence.

"Oh, *jah*," she replied with a smile and a vague wave toward the road. "Close by."

"Guess you get to walk to work, then," he said.

She nodded as she completed his sale. "Most of the people walk somewheres."

He felt he had to keep the conversation going. "So, are there other parks and tourist sites around here?"

"*Jah*," she nodded again. "There's a map over there." She pointed to a rack of flyers and brochures near the door.

Jeremy found maps of both Daviesss and Randolph Counties so he took one of each. "See ya," he said with a wave as he walked out the door. He drove to the designated campsite to set up his RV, unhooking the bronze Kia that he used for traveling. He went inside the camper to get a sandwich from the fridge and to get out his computer. This place had a good view of some woods and he felt he would be able to get some work done, maybe sell a few properties instead of just the one assigned to him. He looked through his portfolio of licenses for Missouri, Illinois, Indiana, Ohio, Michigan, Pennsylvania, Tennessee, Iowa, Wisconsin, and Kentucky. Then he scanned properties available to him for selling. He looked out the window as he made plans for tomorrow. He would drive around the county and look at the properties on the list, focusing on his assignment. He would have to sell the prime listing first, fulfilling his assignment, then he would be free to work on other properties. Fleetingly, his mind went to the young girl who had checked him in. He shook his head to clear his thoughts. "I mustn't get distracted," he said to the air. "One time was enough, wasn't it?"

"Humph!" The Voice snorted. "You've only just begun, Boy! What good is one kill? There are millions of them, out there making more. Besides, your mother needs some new *Kapps*, right? To add to her collection."

Jeremy put his head down on the table. "Why did she start this?"

"To show you the pattern so you could finish it, that's why. I had to be able to help you, right? I couldn't do it while I was still alive, you know."

"We could have been a team," Jeremy whined.

"Wake up! We are a team!"

"Where's Jack, anyway?" Jeremy's voice rose.

"Don't worry about him," The Voice retorted.

"I like it better when I can see you."

"You're in control of that. At least you can hear me and know I'm always with you. Remember, Son, this is practice. There is an ultimate goal, but it will take lots and lots of practice."

Jeremy stood suddenly. "I'm going for a walk," he said as he walked out the door and started along the dusty campground road. "Is this what it feels like to be crazy?" He muttered. "What is the ultimate goal, anyway? What am I supposed to do?" He scratched his head in confusion. "Maybe I need to go back and talk to Ken again, tell him the truth, and…"

"And ruin everything?" The Voice was angry. Dad suddenly stood in the path right in front of Jeremy. "Just calm down, Boy, and get in the practice."

"I'm not exactly a boy," he muttered.

Once the encounter was over, being outside, enjoying plants and animals was soothing. Jeremy walked some woodland trails cut into the woods for the enjoyment of park guests. It would all be fine. "I'll sell the property and go home. I don't need to sell anything else, or spend more time here." He looked around at the trees. "It's pretty and all, but I don't dare stay." The trail ended and he turned around and walked back to his RV. It was still early, but he decided to go to bed anyway. "I'm not hungry, so there's no need to fix anything for supper. I'll just get some sleep so tomorrow can come faster."

And sleep, he did. But, it wasn't the numbing, forgetful sleep he had hoped for. No, this sleep was riddled with dreams of blood and death, some at his hand and some at his mother's. He listened to lessons of killing from The Voice. There was never a body attached in his dreams, just the disembodied voice in his head. He tried to find Dad or Jack, but even though The Voice was still there, he couldn't find them so he could at least make sense of having The Voice speaking to him in the first place. He woke up several times, reminding himself that it was only a dream. But, it never worked to change the dream because the blood and murderous deeds were even more perverse as the night wore on.

At last, it was morning. That is to say, the light from outside was visible and prompted him to get up and do something. He took his clothes and bathed in the park shower house. The water was hot and he used lots of soap to wash off the effects of the dreams. "I have an appointment today," he reminded himself. "An actual buyer," who he would persuade to gain this property. He would alert the national attorney who handled these sales, and the money would be banked. He would get a healthy commission transferred to his own account, from today's efforts, he hoped.

Back at the RV, he looked again at the maps he'd picked up. Fairly jumping off the map at him was a state park, thousands of acres of preserved land, trails, wetlands, and forests.

"It would be perfect," The Voice said.

"I know," he answered by rote. "I know."

He looked at the mileage between where he was and where the state park was located. "It's not that far," he whispered. "But, first things, first. I've got to make this sale. That's what I'm here for, after all."

"Is it?" The Voice wafted off into the air.

"Shut up," Jeremy snarled.

Jeremy chose an apple for his breakfast and went to a local McDonald's for a coffee to go. That would have to do. He arrived early at the property and let himself in with the code he had from the realty association. It was a pretty home in a good neighborhood, on the edge of town. There was a large back yard with a pool and a small shed for equipment. The wood floors shone in the early morning light. Jeremy walked around outside, then locked the door and went to a shopping mall, thinking he might grab a donut or something. He walked around with his roll and juice in hand, as he looked at several shops, one featuring Amish products. "Why am I drawn to this?" He muttered. He walked out of the shop without purchasing anything, got back into his car and drove to the property he was scheduled to sell. He sat outside, in the driveway for nearly two hours, waiting for the prospective buyers. Finally, he let himself into the home and acquainted himself with the features so he could present well and capture the sale. The view from the patio doors, across the privacy fence, was of a peaceful farm scene, a white house with a red barn, cows grazing nearby. He hoped the people were into country living.

He needn't have worried. The sale went smoothly as they oohed and aahed at not only the scenery, but the house and grounds, itself. They set a time to sign the papers, other than the offer to buy, which Jeremy held in his hand. They were thrilled with not only the living space, but the view and the romantic idea of a new start, a new life in a new town. Jeremy smiled at his thoughts. "I don't really care if they have their 'perfect new life,'" he muttered to his rearview mirror, as he backed out of the driveway. "I got the sale, and that means another commission." He was excited about the thought of success. A lazy smile stole across his face, a rarity these days.

He spent a few days driving around the countryside, visiting various historical landmarks, and of course, the state park. He paid for a annual park pass and visited the park daily, driving idly into the campgrounds and walking trails into the woods and swamps. At last, he decided to move his RV into the State Park for the final days of his stay. He pulled in late in the evening on Saturday, paying for a spot for two days. In the trunk of his Kia was a 'gift' he would leave in an obscure part of the park, he had already explored.

Sara

She had to admit it, the Englisher was attractive. There was something about him she found charming. She shook her head to clear her thoughts as she walked on the path across the field. The horses came up to her, one by one, as she passed by, wanting a little attention, hoping for a treat. She patted each one and kept walking. There would be chores to do at home, probably *Mamm* would have dinner about ready and she would help set the table for the family. Sara was a twin to her brother, Samuel, and they were the third and fourth children in a family of nine. She had three older brothers, not counting Samuel, who was only a few minutes older than herself, and she refused to count that, even if he did, and two younger brothers; finally, there were two more girls who had been born. She doted on her two younger sisters as though she was a second mother to them. She couldn't wait to get married and have her own babies to care for. She thought briefly of Caleb, the young Amish man she thought she would someday marry. He had died in a tragic road accident a year ago, and she had not seriously looked at another man. "Until this Englisher comes into the store," she muttered to one of the buggy horses that stretched her neck for more rubbing. "But, I mustn't think of him at all. At least I know I can begin thinking of marriage and a future. I wonder what it will hold? Maybe I'll start going to singings again, too." She smiled at the horse as she continued her walk home.

There were many chores to do. *Mamm* had been sick all day and her sisters had played rather than doing their necessary work. Sara was dismayed. The house needed straitened and supper needed to be made, not even the garden weeding got done this day. "What would they do if I married and left home?" She mourned.

She began by bringing the children all together at the table. "What were you thinking?" She asked in her native tongue. "You should all be *bleched* (punished) for the mess and for not getting the garden done."

"*Mamm* (Mom) was sick," whined Deborah. "Someone had to take care of her."

"*Jah*, and what did you do to take care of her?"

"We left her alone so she could sleep," Josiah piped up. "But," he added. "You wouldn't really whip us, would you?"

Sara had to smile at the innocence. "*Jah*, fine, Josiah, and no, of course I wouldn't. But, now there is much to be done before *Datt* (Dad) and the *Brudders* (brothers) come in from the fields," she reminded them. They didn't need to be told twice, they jumped up and got busy, the boys running to the barn to prepare the milking stalls for the older boys to drive the cows into. Two of the girls attacked the garden weeds, also picking some fresh vegetables for dinner.

Sara washed the day's dishes deciding to cook ham and potatoes for their meal. She watched over those in the house, seeing to it that things got put away, the floors got swept and washed down, and the table set for them all. Finally, she checked on her mother who was awake but weak from a fever.

"Poor Sara," *Mamm* said. "You work all day and come home and do my work."

"Well, just rest, *Mamm*," Sara replied. "Will you come out for supper?"

"*Jah*," *Mamm* nodded. "I think some food would do me good." She pointed to the night stand where stood four cups. "I've had plenty of water, thanks to Josiah and Deborah," she smiled weakly. "My *koppweh* (headache) is nearly gone," she said as she rubbed a hand over her forehead.

"I'll bring it in here," Sara offered.

"No, I'll eat in the kitchen, with the family. Go on, now." She waved her hand to dismiss her oldest daughter.

Sara returned to the kitchen where she prepared the fresh vegetables the girls had deposited in the sink. She made some creamy dressing for the leaf lettuce and set a tray of carrots, onions, radishes, tomatoes, and cucumbers on the table to add to the meal. She took a loaf of homemade bread from the warmer where it had been heating up, adding to the aroma of the ham in the house. She set out a jar of pickles and melted cheese over some crackers and cream, a favorite of her father's.

"Deborah, you and Susanna will do the dishes after we eat," Sara said as they washed up to eat.

"*Dat's* home!" Hollered Josiah.

"Quickly, now!" Sara got them all seated at the trestle table, on their wooden benches.

Sara's twin brother, Samuel, was the first one to the house. "Smells gut in here. *Mamm* must have cooked all day!"

Sara swatted at him as he passed by her. "Are the *bruders* eating with us?" She asked.

"Nah, they went home."

"*Gut* (good), I didn't set them a place, but wasn't sure if you were going back to the fields after supper."

"*Dat's* got a meeting with the Bishop, I think. So, John and Josiah and I are going to clean out the barn after milking."

"I already started," Josiah announced.

"*Jah*, I saw that when I brought the cows in," he tousled the boy's hair with his wet hands.

Josiah beamed at the attention from his older brother.

"Where's *Mamm*?"

"Right behind ya, Son," *Mamm* said as she came into the kitchen.

They all heard the footsteps coming up onto the porch, and, the buggy leaving with their older brothers. Soon *Dat* and John came into the room and washed up for the meal. He kissed his wife before taking his seat at the head of the table. "Feeling better?"

"*Jah*," she answered with a nod.

"Are we in the family way, then?"

All eyes turned to *Mamm*.

"No, Benjamin," she lowered her eyes.

"Well, then," he cleared his throat to indicate the silent prayer for the meal. Another slight cough let them know they could begin passing the food to eat.

All that could be heard for several moments was chewing and the clink of forks on plates, or an occasional burp from one of the boys. At last, *Dat* scooted his chair back, a clear indication that the meal was over. The older children wolfed down whatever was left on their plates, washed it down with milk and scrambled for the door to get the nightly chores done; in the hopes that there would be some free time before dark.

As Sara swept the kitchen, then the porch, she found her thoughts drifting to the young man at the campground. *He seemed kind of nervous and lonely*, she thought. It wasn't often that a single person came to the camp. It was usually families or couples enjoying nature, the trails, and the lake. She wondered what brought him all the way from Pennsylvania to Missouri. She also wondered if he lived in Amish country in Pennsylvania. He didn't seem to stare at her like others did, because of her clothes. And he didn't ask rude questions or ask to take a picture, either. *Maybe he is Amish and he jumped the fence*, she smiled at the thought. *Maybe Gott* (God) *brought him to me to bring him back into the faith.* "Puh!" She said aloud with a long sweep of the broom. She sat in the swing and looked toward *Dat's* big white barn.

A buggy turned into their lane which Sara recognized as the Bishop's before she could clearly see him driving it. His dapple horse trotted proudly down the lane. Sara realized that the Deacon and his son were also with the Bishop and she suddenly wished she weren't so visible. "The last thing I need is a visit from the Deacon's son." She frowned, trying to think how she might slip away unnoticed, but it wasn't to be. They'd seen her, sure enough. Daniel waved and smiled at her.

Sara nodded to acknowledge him, also noticing the smile on the Deacon's face. "It must be some kind of trouble that brings both the Bishop and the Deacon to see *Dat*," she muttered.

"*Gut'n owed* (Good evening), Sara," Daniel said as he stepped up to her.

She smiled again, trying to dodge away, back to the house, to find some work. Yet she also was trying to listen for some tidbit of news, something to tell her what this meeting was about. But, she couldn't hear the muffled words of the older men as they walked away toward the barn. And, Daniel was following close behind her to the porch. She sat in a chair and offered him the swing.

"Have we come at a bad time, Sara?" Daniel asked. He removed his hat and hung it on one knee.

Sara was aware of his intense stare which she found rather unpleasant. It made her feel like one of the bugs or frogs that Josiah often poked and prodded before killing the poor thing with his attention.

"No," she said politely. "Just finished up supper." She refused to look at him, rather inspecting her bare feet on the porch floor. "There might be some pie left," she offered.

"Ate already, but *danki* (thanks)," he said with a bob of his head. "Our fathers are *gut* friends, *jah*?"

Sara looked at the men out by the corral. Her father was petting one of the horses while the deacon talked a mile a minute. She could see the frown on *Dat's* face as he listened. *That doesn't look friendly to me,* she thought. "*Jah*, I suppose so," she muttered. Boldly, she asked, "What are they talking about?" She kept her eyes on the men, noticing the frown on the Bishop's face, as well.

"Not sure I know," Daniel said, his own eyes going to the men. "I think it must be about the missing girl, you know."

"They haven't found Rebekah at all?" She felt sad for the Stoltfus family. She and Rebekah had played together as children, but when they were done with school, it was more difficult to keep a close friendship with someone who lived three miles away.

"No, she just vanished. Do you think she jumped the fence?"

"Rebekah?" She was astonished at the thought. "I don't think so. She was ever so faithful."

"Well, if she went to St. Louis, there's no tellin' where she might be by now. It's been days since she was last seen."

"Did you help with the hunt, Daniel?" Sara asked tenderly. She might not like him as a suitor, but he was a kindly young man.

"*Jah*, I did." He admitted soberly. "They quit lookin' yesterday. Datt just came home and said there'd be no more."

"I'm sorry. It must have been difficult."

"I thought a lot of her," he muttered, his face flaming red.

"Oh, Daniel," she put her hand out toward him. "I didn't know..."

Daniel shook his head. "No matter," he said, his eyes filled with sorrow. "If she left the faith, she wouldn't have been a *gut* wife, you know?"

Silence filled the space between them as they watched their fathers speaking.

"You should be careful, Sara, walking to the campground and being around strangers all the time," he suddenly said.

"Oh, it's not so bad," she said. "I walk across *Dat's* field and not along the road, so I feel safe enough. And I'm almost never alone at the store."

"*Jah*, well if Rebekah could be led away, I reckon anyone could," he said sadly.

"Well, we don't know, Daniel. Maybe there's hope yet."

He nodded, rising up to leave as he noticed the men wandering back to the buggy. "*Vergesst net* (Don't forget about) the Singing this week," he waved as she caught up with his father.

"I won't forget," she muttered as she waved good-bye to him. "I just won't be there."

Her father came up and sat wearily on the swing where Daniel had just been. They both watched the buggy turn to depart up the lane and out on the road.

"Bad news, *Dat*?" She ventured.

"*Jah*," he bobbed his head, giving his long beard a tug. "They found the girl, Rebekah," he said sadly.

"But, that's *gut* news, right? I mean, well, what do you mean, *Dat*?"

"She's gone to be with Jesus," he said quietly.

"Oh, poor Daniel," she said. *I should have been nicer to him. He must not have known. Surely, he would have said.*

"Was… was there an accident, then?" She felt suddenly afraid of the answer. Her father was so solemn.

"Can't be sure," he said. "Is there *kaffi* (coffee), Sara?"

"*Jah*, there is. I'll get you a cup." She rose, went to the kitchen and brought them each a cup of the black brew.

"*Danki, Dachter* (Thanks, Daughter)," he muttered.

Sara blew on her cup and took a sip. She waited patiently, as was their way. No hurrying *Datt*. He was a solemn and careful man, she knew, with his family and especially with the horses he raised. They were always gentle and trained well.

"You'll know soon enough, I expect," *Datt* finally said quietly into his cup. "Seems she was killed."

"Killed?" She asked. *How could that be? No one in the community ever got killed unless there was some kind of accident.* "What do you mean?"

"Ah, tis foreign to us, I agree," he nodded sagely. "Sara, I want you to take one of your *brudders* with you when you go a-walkin.'"

"I only go to work, *Datt*…" she began, but halted when his hand came up to stop her.

"You'll obey, Girl," he said quietly, but firmly. There would be no debating this. "Tisn't safe, I fear."

"May I just say…" she began again.

"*Nee*! (No)" This time *Datt* slapped the arm of the swing with his large, calloused hand. "I will hear no more on this. The girl was murdered, Sara. Murdered on her way home, only a few yards from their driveway, they believe." He swiped his hand over his face, and gave his beard a tug. "I know you cross our own land on your way to the campground, but I fear for ya." His eyes looked sad, bleary like he might cry.

Sara had never seen such a thing; Benjamin Yoder, tearing up. "Yes, *Datt*," she said meekly.

"I'll go with her, *Datt*," her twin offered from the stoop. "And I'll see to it she comes home safe, too." Sara hadn't even noticed when Samuel had joined them. He was sitting quietly on the steps to the porch.

"It's settled, then," *Datt* said. It was the end of the conversation. Sara knew better than to bring it up again.

In the morning, Samuel was waiting for her in the kitchen. *Mamm* had already prepared some pancakes, scrambled eggs and sausage for breakfast. She was making orange juice at the sink. "'Bout time," Sam winked at her.

"Hush, now," *Mamm* said with a swat of her hand toward the boy. Sara stuck out her tongue at him. It was a game between them since they were mere toddlers.

"Did you eat yet?" Sara asked as she began to set the table.

"*Nee*, Datt and John are still out in the barn, debating…"

"Samuel," Mamm said in warning. "Tis not your affair what John and your *D'aad* had to say to one another."

"John wants to marry Barbara Stoltfus," Sam whispered to his sister as he sat down beside her on the long bench along the table.

"*Yah*, I know," she looked at him and nodded.

"Children!" *Mamm* spat out at them, but there was a pleased look in her eye as she, herself, thought of a marriage for one of her children. *I do hope he allows it and is not difficult about the match,* she thought. *It would bring such joy to both our families, but especially to the Stoltfus family as they deal with the death of their daughter.*

Soon enough, the family was together for the meal, the chores for the day were decided, and lunches made for Sara and Samuel so they could walk to their jobs. Samuel worked at a nearby chicken farm, close to the campground.

As they walked across the field, Samuel picked a tall stem of grass and popped it into his mouth as they'd often seen their father and older brothers do. "You'll be late for work," Sara commented.

"*Jah*, I will," Sam nodded. "But, Ted won't mind. He knows what's bin goin' on."

"It's sad. Daniel must be *grank* (sick), now that he knows."

Sam scratched his head beneath his straw hat. "Why would Daniel be sick? I thought he liked you?"

Sara waved her hand at him impatiently. "I used to think so, too. But, really he liked Rebekah." She paused as they climbed over the style on the fence. "Do you know what happened to her? Did she suffer?"

"Best not to know all that, Sara," Sam replied.

"Maybe she just fell and…" she stopped at his stern look. "Sometimes you look just like *Datt,* did you know that?" She laughed.

As they continued on, Sara became confused about the situation with Rebekah. She stopped walking as she said, "If she was killed near to home, why'd it take so long to find her?"

Samuel turned around to peer at his sister. "I dunno," he shrugged, but his eyes gave him away. She could always tell by his eyes.

"You know something, I don't, I'll wager," she accused.

"Just that they found the body at the State Park, not near home. I guess the police figured out she was killed here and put out there." He waved his hand for emphasis.

"What the world?" She pondered aloud.

"I dunno, Sara. But, that's why Datt's so worried about us walking alone, you know."

Sam insisted on walking her into the camp store before going on to the chicken farm where he worked. She watched him walk out to the highway and turn to walk along the edge of the road. "I wonder if he's safe," she mused before turning to the counter and setting up her work area. She noticed that there had already been several campsites that were now empty. As she worked, she noted other campers pulling out, going on to their various homes or on with the trip they were started upon. "I'm going out to check the sites!" She called toward the office.

"It's already handled," her boss said. "Just dust the shelves in here and restock some of the supplies. You'll probably get to go home early. Too bad you don't have a phone, I would have told you not to come in. It's going to be a lazy week, I think."

"Already?" She thought about the length of the camping season and that they didn't usually slow down this early, not until closer to Hallowe'en. She went about her duties quietly, only taking a little over an hour, signed out on the register, and said good-bye to the store owner. He was a serious man with not much to say on a regular basis, so it surprised her when he called after her.

"Hey!" He yelled as she was about to walk out the door. "Did you know that dead girl they found? The Amish one, you know."

Sara looked back at him in dismay. *Englishers could be so rude,* she thought. She bobbed her head, "*Jah,*" she replied.

"Too bad about that," he went on. "Who'd want to kill an Amish girl?"

Who, indeed, she questioned, but only shrugged and shook her head.

"Well, it had to be a stranger," he persisted in a gossipy tone. "Amish don't kill Amish, from what I know." He peered at her as though she might give him information.

"I really don't know," she said quietly, wishing he would end the conversation.

"Was she jumping the fence?" He asked too eagerly.

The question caught her off-guard. "Wh-what?" She stammered.

"Well, you know, her *Kapp* being missing and all," he explained with a gesture toward her own *Kapp* on her head.

How would an Englisher know such a thing? She thought, panic rising in her throat. "I, uh, I really don't know much about what happened to Rebekah.

"Thought you folks had that Amish grapevine and knew all the news," he chuckled.

Sara looked at him in confusion. It was the most she had ever heard him speak, let alone laughing. Usually, his wife did all the talking.

"Any campers left at all?" She asked to change the subject.

"Nope, but that guy from Pennsylvania said to tell you good-bye. Guess you made a good impression on him."

Sara felt her face get warm at the words. "Just try to do my job," she mumbled.

"Well, it's good for business," he said. "Fella said he wanted to spend a few days at the State Park or some other place, but that he might come back because of you." He turned back to his office. "Keep checking your phone shanty. I'll leave a message if I need you on the weekend."

Sara waved as she stepped out the door. "*How odd*," she thought. Sara decided to stop at the poultry farm to let Samuel know she was leaving early. His boss told her he was busy, so she didn't get to talk to him. "Just let him know I've gone on home early, would you please?"

"Sure, I'll try to remember to tell him when I see him."

Sara wondered if she should just hang around and wait until lunch time to tell him herself, but decided that it was broad daylight and she could safely walk home alone, as she did nearly every day. As she approached the fence, she realized that the stallion was out in the field with the mares. He could be ornery and she was a little afraid of him, so she decided, just this once, to walk down the main highway to their road to get home. "I won't speak to any strangers," she told herself, looking carefully for traffic as she walked onto the side of the paved road. It was about half a mile to the dirt road that ran right by their house, another half mile to the north. "I'll be fine," she assured herself, walking swiftly as cars and trucks zoomed past her on their way to who knows where.

When a car slowed and stopped just ahead of her, Sara stopped, afraid to walk on. It was a little Kia and looked familiar, but she didn't know any Englishers other that those who lived near her community. The plate said Pennsylvania.

Jeremy stepped out of his car along the highway as soon as there was a lull in the traffic. "Need a ride?" He asked with a smile.

Anna couldn't help but smile. "It's only a little ways," she pointed across the field to her right.

"Still, I can take you and you won't have to walk." He ran around and opened the passenger door for her.

"Well, *Datt*, that is, my father, wouldn't be pleased," she said, walking closer to him. He smelled like some kind of spicy fruit. It was a good smell. "I thought you left the area," she added.

"I did, but I like driving around the countryside. If I hadn't, I wouldn't have run into you again." He smiled, waving his hand for her to get into the car.

Sara shook her head. "I shouldn't, really, but I appreciate the offer."

"It's the least I can do for someone who treated me so well at the campground," he persisted.

Anna felt a slight prickle of alarm, although she couldn't figure out why she should. He had always been kind to her, too. She pointed at the white farmhouse across the field. "No, tis right over there. I'd best not."

Jeremy leaned against his car. "How come a pretty girl like you isn't married already?" He asked.

Anna blushed. "Well, I doubt I will ever marry," she said softly. "Not planning to, right now."

"Still lots of time for marriage and babies, right?" He went on.

"Not for me," she said. Crossing toward the fence, she waved. "I need to be getting home. *Mamm* isn't well and I need to care for her," she lied with a shake of her head. She truly felt afraid, with no good reason. She hurried on, turning to look back only once. For the first time, she noticed that he held some kind of tool in his hand. She felt like running, but just kept walking, close to the fence, even though it was harder to walk in the tall grass and weeds. At last, she heard the car speed away, and saw with relief, that it was going down the highway at a high rate of speed. She suddenly realized she had been holding her breath. When he didn't turn on their road, she let out a loud whoosh of air and stopped to calm her frazzled nerves.

She made her way to the county road, picked up the hem of her skirt, and ran as fast as she could for their lane. Her *Kapp* came loose, so she yanked it off, hairpins flying everywhere. She didn't care, she just wanted to get home. As she turned into the lane, she slowed down, looking back over her shoulder once again. The little car was not in sight. Sara bent over and took several deep breaths. At last, she walked toward the house. The peaceful scene warmed her heart, tears spilling down her cheeks. *Datt was right,* she thought. *The world is unsafe for any of the people. I must never go alone anywhere again.*

Jeremy couldn't believe the girl shunned him like she did. He knew she was attracted to him, could see it in her eyes. He grabbed the bat from the front seat when she walked over to the fence. "It can't be done here," he mumbled. "Too much traffic." He watched her for a few moments as she scurried away, her dress and feet tangling in the weeds. *She knows,* he thought. *Somehow, she knows.* "That's malarkey," Dad said. "She knows nothing. She's just another girl who will grow up and make more girls."

"Shut up!" Jeremy spat. "Let me decide, for once!" *She said no babies or marriage for her. Maybe there are some girls who are safe,* Jeremy thought. *Maybe everyone doesn't have to be 'practice.' Maybe I can make the decisions now.*

"More malarkey," Dad said quietly. "Are you gonna do this or not?"

"Not," Jeremy threw the bat into the car, shut the door, and sped away.

Kentucky and Tennessee

Jeremy drove through Kentucky and Tennessee, looking at some of the properties listed there. He wasn't impressed with what he saw. Most of it was raw land with some shack on it or an old mobile home. "I can't sell something like that," he muttered. He drove for miles through picturesque countryside, heading into the Smokey Mountains. He didn't see any Amish farms anywhere, which pleased him. What he did see was a lot of poverty. Once he got off the main highways, he was amazed at the poor living conditions. He drove through some towns that he thought must be abandoned, but astonishingly, he saw children playing in the empty buildings, and witnessed a few families here and there. "This isn't for me," he said. "I need to get back out on a major highway and find some high dollar properties to sell. My commission on this, would be zero or less." He smiled at his little joke.

He stopped at a gas station that still had an attendant pumping gas. As he sat in his car, a teenaged girl came up to his window. "Hey, Mister, can you give me a lift?"

"No!" He said, looking into his rearview mirror, checking to see if Dad or Jack were there.

"I just need to get over them hills over there," she pointed with a popsicle stick she had been sucking on.

"Get away from there, Meghan," the attendant said. "The fella said no, so git on down the road your own self."

Meghan, if that was her name, smiled beautifully before flipping her coal-black hair and walking away.

"Sorry about that, Mister. She don't have no manners, no how."

"It's okay," Jeremy said. "How much do I owe you?"

"$18.50, so says my old pump," the man smiled to reveal missing and broken teeth. "Do you want the oil checked?"

"No, it's fine," Jeremy paid the attendant $20.00. "Keep the change," he said as he began closing his window.

"Hey, thanks!" The man smiled again.

Jeremy drove down the street looking for a sign to the freeway. Standing beside it, was the girl, Meghan. She waved at him, with a big smile. Jeremy looked in his rearview mirror. His was the only car in sight. Carefully, he rolled down the window. "You are persistent," he said with a nervous smile. *Is this some kind of trap?* He thought.

"No, it's a gift," countered the Voice.

"I knew you'd be along, sooner or later," she said, walking toward the car. "Want to give me a lift somewhere?"

"Isn't that dangerous?" He asked. "You don't know me."

"Yeah, that's the point. I know everyone else around here, and they won't take me anywheres."

"I'm a real estate broker, going to Lexington, then to Knoxville," he said, hitting the unlock button for the passenger door.

"Great!" She opened the door and flung her backpack into the back seat. "The only way I have to pay you is, well, you know."

"What are you going to do in Lexington, prostitute yourself?"

She shrugged. "That's mostly what I do here, so why not? I get a job here and there, but nothing much."

"No family?"

"Don't get to know her," the Voice warned.

"Sure, Mama has a passel of kids." She lied, looking out the window at the passing scenery. "Reckon I will too, one day. But, for now, I'm all about having fun and seeing something besides these hills!"

Jeremy pulled off on a side road.

"Hey, where you going?" She asked, sitting up straight in her seat. "This doesn't go to Lexington."

"Remember? I'm looking for properties for sale, real estate. I didn't say I was going straight to Lexington."

She frowned, concern showing plainly on her fact. "Oh, yeah," she mumbled.

Jeremy carefully turned on back roads until he came to a dead end with an old miner's shack and a gravel pit. He drove slowly onto a rocky parking area. "Hmmm," he said, getting out of the car, his little bat in his hand. He was sure the girl would follow.

She didn't disappoint him. "This don't look like much," she said.

He looked at her, measuring the distance. "Run," he said quietly.

"What?" She looked suddenly frightened. "No!" She yelled as she began to make the turn and sprint toward the shack. But, it was too late. The bat hit her squarely between the eyes, almost imbedding itself in her skull. She dropped quietly to the ground.

Jeremy walked carefully on the rocks to retrieve his bat, then went back to the car and used some Clorex Wipes to clean it. He stuffed the soiled wipes into her backpack, where he discovered a brown, leather tam. "Huh," he muttered. "A little hat." He placed the hat on the floor of the passenger seat, threw the backpack into the dust near her feet, and got into his car. He whistled a little tune he'd heard earlier on the radio as he retraced his route back to the freeway. "Freeway," he laughed out loud. "Whoever came up with that name?" He laughed again. "Free, way," he said. "It's a little joke, right? I'm free, and I'm on my way."

"Don't be so cocky," Dad said from the back seat.

Jeremy looked in his rearview mirror, into the face he loved. "Like you said, it was a gift."

"It doesn't always have to be about hats, Jerr," Dad growled. "That might have been a mistake.

"Nah, that was just a bonus," he snickered.

Once in Lexington, he had to work hard to sell two properties in a suburb. But, it was worth the effort. After about a month, the sales were final and he could be on his way to Knoxville, Tennessee. He looked forward to the change. He was bored with Lexington, horses, and blue grass country. He hadn't really seen much of the surrounding area, other than driving to the houses and meeting people at the Country Club. He spent most of his time at the motel, swimming and using their exercise equipment. The leather tam laid on his desk for a week before he decided what to do about it. He carefully cut off the band around the front and put it away into his suitcase with the *Kapp* strings he had 'collected' on this trip. Then he wrote a short quip for his mother, packed the hat in a box and sent it to her. "She'll be really surprised with this one," he chuckled as he taped the box up and wrote her address on top. He packed the *Kapps* he'd gotten into another box and sealed it up, too. "I'll mail this one in a week or so, after she gets the little brown one." He smiled at himself in the full-length mirror on the bathroom door. "I'd love to see her face when she opens it up."

Jeremy dressed well. Working with bankers and lawyers gave him a sense that he was important and he needed to look the part. He rarely wore suits, but he did go for a more dressed-up, casual look, as he liked to call it. He spent a lot of time on his hair, making sure it was perfectly combed and stayed in place. He knew his appearance helped in making sales. "No one wants to do business with a bum," he often reminded himself, although he never looked like 'a bum', by any stretch of the imagination. His final three days in Kentucky was spent with a lawyer, a banker, and another real estate agent, all of whom one of the purchasing couples has hired. Jeremy felt pressured, like he was being scrutinized. He could barely look the lawyer in the face, but forced himself to be calm so he could finalize this sale.

"Everything seems to be in order," the lawyer said as he looked through every piece of paper once again. "Your credentials are valid," he stared hard at Jeremy. Finally, he closed the folder of papers and looked again at Jeremy. "I can't help but think that I'm missing something," he said.

Jeremy looked up at the lawyer, then down at his own folder with copies of everything in it. "I'm sure everything is in there," he stated simply. "I have made many sales of this sort, and I can assure you I'm a very careful man."

The lawyer smiled sardonically. "I'm sure you are." He said. "Perhaps that's what has me 'on edge', so to speak. This is a lot of money, but it is also a lot of house..." He paused, twirling a pen in his hand. Looking at the banker, he said, "Well, George, I suppose it is signable. Go ahead and make the loan to the buyer." He looked again at Jeremy. "Where are you going from here?"

"What?" Jeremy was startled. "Well," he flashed a big smile. "I have another sale in Tennessee, so I guess it's on to there." He clasped his hands on top of his folder, hoping he looked calmer than he felt. *What is this man looking for? What does he know?* Jeremy thought.

But, he held his head high, kept a half smile on his face.

"So, all you do is travel around selling properties? Why couldn't Mr. Emmson, here, sell it, and not you?"

Again, Jeremy smiled. "I don't know why it wasn't sold previously," he looked briefly at the agent, "but it was on the national listing and I was the lucky salesman."

The lawyer scrutinized Jeremy again; indeed, he barely left off staring at him. "According to this contract, a check will be sent to the national board that regulates your sales. They are, I believe, in Cincinnati, Ohio."

"Yes," Jeremy nodded. He'd almost said "sir," but felt it would have made him seem like a little boy talking to the headmaster at school.

"And, evidently, they pay you."

Again, Jeremy nodded. "That is correct. My commission will be transferred to my bank account in a week or two after they receive the funds from you." He indicated the three other men at the table.

The banker shut his portfolio loudly, latched it, and stood to leave. "I believe, then, we are done here. Everyone has signed the documents and the house is sold."

Jeremy slowly let out the breath he had been holding.

"I'm not sure I like what you do," the lawyer said, as he too, rose to leave.

"What?" Jeremy's mouth went dry. He looked up at the man who seemed to tower over him menacingly.

"I just think there is a better way to do what you do."

Jeremy frowned as his mind swirled with visions of hats and girls.

"Steady, Son," said Dad. "Hear him out before you panic."

"I think these local sales should be handled locally, not by some stranger who comes in and out, never to be seen again." He paused, looking at Jeremy as though he was a bug on the carpet. "I shall see about this organization and it's need in our state." He shook his head as he walked toward the door. "Maybe I'm looking for ghosts," and the door closed behind him.

Jeremy was alone in the room. He felt sick to his stomach with the release of adrenaline that had built up from his rising panic.

"See?" Dad said. "All he was interested in was the stupid sales stuff. You were all riled up for nothing. You gotta get ahold of yourself, Boy."

"Shut up!" Jeremy slid his chair back as he stood. In three strides he was out the door, and in five more, at the elevator. He couldn't wait to get out to his car.

It took less than three hours to get to the new motel where he set up his portable office. He began making calls to get access to properties. There was only one home listing that was what he was looking for, and he made arrangements to get the keys so he could tour the mansion on the edge of town. Someone had built it, then couldn't afford to live in it. "Fate lends a hand," he said aloud in the emptiness. This would be a high-dollar home after he hired a cleaner, because it was dusty and a few spiders had been busy building webs among the chandeliers. He went back to the motel to make the necessary arrangements.

Jeremy was a meticulous and careful man. He made clear, concise notes about each home, his dealings with prospective buyers, and his accounting of costs and commissions. He reviewed his neat, print-style handwriting with pride. Last of all, he turned to his journals. He kept one of how life should be, and one of what happened on a daily basis. Lastly, he kept a notebook of his 'secrets'. "Someday, Mother will know what she started, and how Dad and I have been able to carry out the quest." He sat back in the armchair as he leafed through his journal. It only had a few pages written on, but everything he and Dad talked about was there. He briefly wondered about Jack because he never saw or heard from him anymore. "We don't need him anymore, Son," Dad commented. Idly, Jeremy fingered the *Kapp* strings and the leather strap, he had collected. He would always remember the first one, the one with the pizza sauce stain, and linger over the feel of that first time successfully using his little bat. He laid his head back in the chair, closed his eyes, and ran the string through his fingers, over and over. *It's no longer frightening,* he thought. *I'm content to have done this for her.*

"What do you mean, 'for her?'" Dad said in a loud voice.

Jeremy sat up observing that his father was standing across the room. "I've added to her collection," Jeremy said weakly.

"Isn't this about ridding the world of her?" Dad asked.

"Of people like her," Jeremy whispered. "Not her."

Dad snorted in disgust. "What do you think the goal is here, Jerr…" He only used the nickname when he was upset or treating Jeremy like a child these days.

"I don't know." He said. "Some vendetta of yours, I guess."

"Really," Dad observed sarcastically.

For the first time in a very long while, Jeremy had the vision of his mother, covered in blood, standing over his father with a knife in her hand. Even today, it brought tears to his eyes. "What did she do to Jack?" He wondered aloud. He remembered the blood on the floor, under the desk, in his mother's home. "How did she get rid of the body before I came home from school?" He envisioned her digging a hole in the backyard, *maybe even in the little woods,* he shuddered. "I spent so much time out there and didn't know," he whimpered.

Another vision crossed his mind, one of a woman, looking exactly like Jack, driving Jack's old Jeep, haunted him. "It must have been his twin sister, or something," Jeremy stated. "Did she know what happened to Jack? Should I have talked to her?" He firmly shook his head. "No, just another woman to lie to me, probably."

Jeremy woke up with a start, rubbing his neck. He'd fallen asleep in the chair, which was not made for sleeping. He stood up to stretch his arms and legs, twisting the kinks out of his back and neck. The strings, in their plastic bag, fell to the floor.

Jeremy showered, before going out for supper. He found a quiet diner where he could eat alone and not be noticed by others for doing so. He felt that when he ate alone at a classy restaurant, he was scrutinized by others. In a diner, no one seemed to care. He watched people come and go, spending some time watching a couple having an argument out on the sidewalk. He idly wondered if the woman would go home and murder her friend in the middle of the night. She was screaming and seemed threatening. All of that stopped when the man got into a pickup truck and sped away. The woman laughed as he drove off and, somehow, that angered Jeremy. It was only a few steps to his car where he grabbed the bat. In the semi-darkness of the parking lot, he watched the woman head for her own pickup truck. One, carefully aimed throw, and she dropped to the ground. Jeremy looked around the parking lot. It was busier than he realized and he felt a tendril of fear.

"Stupid, Boy!" Dad yelled at him.

"Shut up!" He snapped back. "Let me do what I need to do." He walked around the perimeter of the parking lot to the truck. It was at least four car widths from the nearest light. Jeremy saw his bat sticking straight up out of her head. "A clean shot again," he whispered with a contented smile. It was as he was bending over to retrieve his bat, that he realized the woman was wearing a scarf with strings splayed on the pavement. He pulled it from beneath her head and stuffed it into his shirt. He walked to a grassy spot near the fence where he wiped his bat off with dirt and grass. Then we went for a walk down the street to another restaurant where he sat over a very long cup of coffee. It took him so long that he was able to watch the commotion of emergency vehicles at the diner. The police had cordoned off about half of the parking lot as a "crime scene." Jeremy walked around about four blocks to come toward the parking lot from the opposite side. "What's going on over there?" He asked a bystander.

"Millie got herself killed," the man said. "Clyde probably finally done her in. It's been comin' on for a long time now."

Jeremy shook his head. "Do you think they'd mind if I took my car? I've been down there at the river walk and would like to go home now."

"Nah, I don't think so. We were eating at the diner and they won't let us leave. And we walked here!"

Jeremy sat quietly in his car, hoping they didn't talk to him. He slid the scarf and the bat slowly under his seat. He didn't have to wait long. A couple of uniformed officers soon began clearing the area outside the yellow tape, of bystanders and gawkers. He was waved ahead, out of the parking lot and the lights. He heard the man he was talking to explaining to the police that the woman and her husband had been fighting when he suddenly pulled away, fast. He smiled at the distortion of details. That fight had taken place right outside the diner and the woman had died clear at the back side of the parking lot. "We did it again." He acclaimed. "Got Mom another hat and me another string. I'll cut that off and stick the scarf in the box with the others," he thought for a moment. "Nope, I'll send the scarf in its own envelope. Another surprise." He chuckled as he drove off into the night. Tennessee was turning out to be a good place already.

The sales he made became a part-time job. He spent his time trolling for Amish settlements in the area. He was not disappointed. There were a few good-sized communities for him to watch and learn the habits of the local women. He managed to sell two properties and when he drove back into Kentucky, two new *Kapps* rested neatly in the trunk of his car. It was finally time to go back to Pennsylvania, but not before he made a detour into Missouri, Illinois, and Indiana. He only sold one more home, but the commission would be a nice one. His focus was more directed toward Amish communities and the possibilities of more *Kapps* for his mother.

At a motel in Ohio, his father began haranguing him into an argument. "Have you forgotten what this is all about, Son?"

"Leave me alone," Jeremy growled.

"We're back in Ohio. It's time to go see your mother."

"Not yet," Jeremy was almost in tears.

"Don't give me that baby act again," Dad sat on the end of the bed shaking his head sadly.

"I've got more to do," Jeremy began.

"Really?" Dad paused. "When's that going to end so we can finish the job we started out to do?"

"Why don't you do it yourself?"

Dad laughed. "Well, if that's not obvious, you're crazy!"

Jeremy was rubbing the heels of his hands along his cheeks, when he stopped and looked up. "Am I? Am I crazy?"

"Depends," Dad answered.

"Were you mentally ill, Dad? I was told you were."

"Don't worry about that now," Dad was getting edgy. "Focus on the job, okay?"

"If I can see and hear you and Jack, then am I mentally ill, too?" Jeremy wondered out loud.

"Focus!" Dad yelled.

Jeremy ignored him and contemplated what it meant to be mentally ill. "I don't feel sick," he said. "I feel normal." He paused. "What is normal, anyway?" No answer.

"Did Mom kill you because you were sick?" Still no answer. "Was Jack sick, too?" He shook his head as he laid back on the bed. He tried to remember what he saw as a child. He pictured the dining room and his hiding spot under the table among the chair legs. Dad was screaming and Mom was yelling, too. "No, no, no…" he whimpered into his hands. He cried into one of the pillows on the bed until it was wet with his tears. "Why did she grab that knife? Why did she kill you?" he laid quietly with his eyes tightly shut. "At least she killed Jack while I was at school."

"Are you done yet?" Dad asked in a bored voice.

"Yeah, he's such a whiner," Meghan said.

Jeremy put the pillow over his head. *Why is she here? Why is Dad allowing her to be here?* He peeked out, but no one was in the room. Darkness was creeping across the landscape outside, so he quickly turned on the bedside lamp. "How is it even possible that she can come into my thoughts? I didn't know her." He pictured again the perfect kill shot he made with his bat. "And why is Dad allowing it?" He sat up, yelling into the gathering dusk outside the window. "Don't come back! I don't need you! I've shown you what I can do! I can do more, too! I don't need you anymore!" Silence greeted him. He fell into an exhausted slump on the bed.

When morning came, he was sore all over, having thrashed around on the bed most of the night, not getting any good sleep. He stretched out his full length on the bed, his feet dangling in the air. He had slept in his clothes, so they were wrinkled, "And I smell like a pig sty," he commented. But, he didn't get up just yet. He put his hands behind his head, staring up at the ceiling. A plan was formulating; something sinister to some, maybe, but he smiled as thoughts became visions of all the *Kapps* he would start sending to his mother. He got up and rummaged through his briefcase for paper and a pencil. He took out his computer, set it up, stretched again, then got out his clean clothes before going into the bathroom to shower.

In the shower, he imagined the water was blood. He reveled in being able to let the 'blood' run over his body and down the drain. The whiteness of his body soap made the vision stop, but he smiled as he basked in the memory. A vision of his mother, soaked in blood, flooded his mind. "I've become just like her," he said as he began to dry off.

No, you haven't," Dad said from his seat on the toilet. "I had you do some practice, and now it's time to end this."

Jeremy smiled again. "You aren't real and I don't have to listen to you and your friends." He put the towel over his shoulder as he walked into the bedroom to dress completely. The computer was ready to use, giving him a sense of control. Another smile crossed his handsome face.

An hour later, he had a crude map drawn of his 'target states.' He brought up houses for sale in each of them, so he could have a legitimate excuse for traveling to each state. But, he wasn't planning on doing much house hunting or selling. On his map, he marked Amish communities, his real targets for this trip. "My final spree," he muttered; somehow knowing this would be his last trip.

He picked up his phone to call his mother. She answered on the first ring. "Jeremy, is that you?"

"Of course it's me. What's going on? You sound upset."

"No, I, oh well you know, I just haven't heard from you in a while..." she fumbled with the words.

"Didn't you get my packages?"

Silence for a few seconds. "Yes, Son, I got them."

"You don't like them," he accused.

"It's not that, I, uh, well, they're all so different, and..."

"I knew you'd be surprised," he laughed. "I wish I could have seen your face."

Anna took a big breath. "Jeremy, where are you right now?"

"Uh, why?"

"I just wondered if you're coming home anytime soon."

"You mean to your house? The answer is, no. I am going home to Pennsylvania in a couple of weeks, though."

"Through Ohio, but not stopping by, is that it?" She sounded so whiney to his ears.

"Hey, look Mom, I've gotta run. I'll invite you and grandma over some time, okay?"

"Jeremy, please come home. I want to see you. I'm worried about you."

He felt a sudden panic. *What does she know?* "What's going on, Mom? You're acting suspicious."

"Suspicious?" She swallowed hard. "Jeremy, I'm the Mom, and I love you. I have every right to worry." She paused. "Won't you come home? Are you close enough to come here for a day, at least?"

"Nope!" He couldn't put his finger on it, but there was something going on. "No, I'm not coming there. Not now. See ya'!" And with that he hung up the call.

He looked hard at his map, then circled central Ohio, her home. "Yeah, I'll come there sometime, Mom," he muttered. "I've got some more work to do before that day comes." He idly tapped the map with his pen.

The Killing Spree

It began in Holmes County, OH. Jeremy awoke on Friday morning to a sunny sky. He meticulously packed his clothes in his suitcase, dressed up in his favorite pants and polo shirt, and carefully packed his car. He took a sheet of painter's plastic for a lining in the trunk of his car, placing all his personal belongings into the back seat. Breathing deeply of the refreshing morning air, he walked back into the motel where he ate a hearty breakfast, reading the local paper with seeming interest. After eating, he walked to the parking lot and inspected the outside of his car. A spot of dirt caught his eye and he paused to clean it off. Jeremy always liked his things to be neat and tidy.

When he started up the engine, he sat for a few minutes to scroll through calls and texts on his phone. He engaged the Bluetooth headset for his phone and checked on his little metal bat. It was tucked neatly under the passenger's seat. He drew it out, fingering it lovingly. At last, he felt he was ready. He put the car into gear and pulled out of the parking lot, headed out of town into the countryside for the first victim of his finale. He chuckled at the term.

"Why are you doing this?" Dad asked from the backseat. "Just go take care of your mother and be done with the whole thing."

Jeremy looked meaningfully into the rearview mirror. "There's time for that. It will be the end, but for now, I'm on a mission. Lots of practice, remember?" He paused as he drove into the country. "Now," he said calmly. "Leave me alone. I told you I don't need you anymore. Go away."

"I thought we were a team," Dad whined.

Jeremy took a long, measured breath. "Not anymore. I will finish this. Maybe I really never needed you in the first place. Maybe this has always been my calling, my destiny." He slowed down to turn onto a dirt road, into the heart of Amish country. At a small village, he stopped at the general store and bought some candy, eyeing the customers in the store. Two teenaged girls were giggling together in the corner. One of them wore a shawl, so he supposed she would be leaving soon. He paid for his treat and walked out onto the porch. A couple of gray-beards were playing a game of checkers near a window. He watched for a moment, then went to his car, munching on the hard candies he had bought. He leaned on the hood, looking at a map of Ohio. It was a ploy he had often used successfully. It gave him time to wait, to watch without seeming too conspicuous.

Suzanna walked out onto the porch and spoke in her native tongue to the men seated there. "*Wer ist siegreich?*" *(*Who is winning),

"Josiah, *gewissdoch!*" (of course)

She laughed. "*Wie er es gewöhnlich macht!*" (As he usually does)

"*Jah, ich glaube, das tut er,*" (Yes, I guess he does). They all laughed heartily together.

Suzanna turned to go, waving at the two men. "*Guder nammidaag,*" (Good afternoon).

"*Grüßen Sie Ihren Vater von mir!*" (Remember me to your father). The older of the two men waved back at her, his long, white beard wagging against his chest.

"*Jah, ich will,*" (Yes, I will) she answered with another wave.

Suzanna glanced at the stranger getting into his shiny car. He smiled at her, giving her a little wave as he started the engine. She walked down the steps and onto the dusty driveway. Turning toward the hitching rail, she walked up to two horses standing in the sunlight. Speaking softly to them, she watched as the car backed out and headed down the road toward the highway. Suzanna stepped out onto the dirt with her bare feet and hurried down the road in the opposite direction. Her plum colored dress rustled as she rushed forward. She wasn't sure why she felt fear, but she recognized that she did. It was a two-mile walk across the fields and about a three mile walk along county roads, to her home. She decided to walk along the dirt road so she could step down into the creek near the old, wooden bridge so she could enjoy the cool water on her feet. The bridge was on an intersecting road which led to her father's large farm. As she approached the road, she climbed slowly down the bank toward the water. Stepping into the water, she watched in amusement as fish darted away from her. A gleam in the water caught her attention. There was a broken shell, and another nearby. She began looking for unique stones, losing track of time and distance as she wandered along the sandy creek. Suzanna looked up suddenly, becoming aware that she had better be heading home or her father would be angry because of her wasting time. "Again," she sighed softly.

She didn't even hear the bat whirring through the air, as it hit her in the temple. She dropped into the water with a splash.

Jeremy walked calmly down to the creek's edge to retrieve his bat and the precious *Kapp* for his mother. He stuffed them both into a jacket pocket as he turned to walk back to his car. "Suzanna! Oh, Suzanna!" He heard someone yell from the bridge only a short distance upstream. Panic seized him for a moment. Two young girls came running to the dead girl. A third child ran in the opposite direction. Jeremy backed away from the water as they approached. "What happened?" One of them looked up at him. "Did you see what happened?"

"No, uh, I just saw the body there and came to investigate." His palms were sweaty, and his voice had an odd tenor to it. "I, uh, I think she fell and hit her head on a rock or something."

The girls began to cry, but they dragged their sister from the water onto the sandy shoal, turning her over to reveal the gash and indentation in her head.

Jeremy backed up further, turned abruptly, then fled to his car. He crammed the bat and *Kapp* under the passenger seat, climbed into the driver's seat, and drove away, remembering not to speed. "Slow and steady," he mumbled. "Just get away from here."

Benjamin Schlabach stepped carefully through the water to the sandbar where his oldest daughter lay. Martha and Rebecca looked up at him in sorrow, tears streaming down their faces. He became conscious of details; how the water soaked half-way up their dresses, their bare feet, Suzanna's bare feet, fish swimming in the water as the sun sparkled off the surface of it. *Just like nothing happened here,* he thought. "*Was wird heir gespleit?*" (What's going on here?) He asked.

"*Sie fiel.*" (She fell). Rebecca said.

"*Sie hit seinen Kopf.*" (She hit her head). Martha replied at the same time.

Benjamin grunted in reply, still surveying the area. The creek here was sandy bottomed. There were few rocks of any size, most were pebbles or small stones, not nearly large enough to account for the hole he could plainly see in her temple. He stooped down to look at the wound. "Was ist das?" (What is this?) He murmured. Gently, he lifted her into his arms and walked toward the bridge and their home about a half mile away. He turned, looking back to survey the creek once more, shaking his head, his beard brushing softly across her head which lay against his chest. Her wet, loose hair swung gently with each step.

By the time they got home, the Bishop was already arriving. He got out of his buggy as Benjamin laid his daughter on the porch. His wife was crying silently, wringing her hands in her green choring apron, waiting for the men to pronounce what she could clearly see. Soon, very soon, others would be arriving to help. The Amish grapevine runs swiftly and smoothly with information, from house to house. She had already sent her youngest son to spread the news.

"*Sie ist tödlich verunglückt?*" (She was killed in an accident?) The Bishop asked as he looked down at the still form in her plum-colored dress.

Benjamin was instructing his older boys to get saw horses from the barn and put them in the sitting room inside. He knew a coffin would be arriving soon. It was the way of the People to take care of one another, to anticipate a need before it was evident. "*Ich bin mir nicht sicher.*" (I'm not sure.) He replied.

The Bishop drew his large, bushy eyebrows together in a frown. "*Und was dann?*" (Then what?)

Benjamin wiped his hands over his face, wiping away the tears that were falling onto his full beard. "*Ich weiß nicht.*" (I don't know.) He pointed at the wound on her face, now purple and swollen. "*Das sehe siel einer an!*" (Just look at that!)

"Hmmmm," the Bishop wagged his old head.

The day of the funeral, Rebecca cried to her father, telling him about the man who said Suzanna had fallen and hit her head. She described him as an "Englisher," driving a yellow car. She could only remember that he was "old" and "had on a blue shirt." Martha didn't remember him at all. Had there really been someone there? Benjamin had heard some stories… but, surely they were safe here in the heart of the People. He couldn't imagine outsiders coming here, to their remote country roads. Still, he couldn't sleep, barely ate, and was falling behind in his work. He hadn't cried since being a small child. Not like this, this non-stop weeping and shaking of his very frame. A week after the funeral, and against advice from his Bishop, he made a call to the police. A very nice detective came to visit with him and they walked to the creek. He pointed to the sandbar near the center of the creek, jutting out into the rushing water.

"How was she laying in the water?" Detective Jones asked.

"I don't know," Benjamin rubbed his face to rid himself of the memories. "My younger girls found her and pulled her up onto the sand." He paused, staring into the sparkling water. His voice became husky as he fought with his emotions. "She had a wound on the side of her face, like she'd hit her head on something." He pointed to his own temple, and swallowed hard. "Maybe she hit a rock or a stick, or other debris in the water."

The detective looked all around. It was sandy here, no rock big enough to cause a fatal wound, that he could see. Water and debris change all the time, so he couldn't pinpoint anything that might have been a cause of death like the bereaved father was talking about. "Did you see something she might have landed on?" He asked.

"*Nein* (no)," Benjamin said, slowly moving his head from side to side. "I just can't figure out how she fell in the first place."

"How did the girls find her?" The detective was sorrowful that he hadn't been called right away, but understood they thought it was an accident. He also had lived and worked long enough in this area to know the Amish don't easily call upon the law to help with their matters.

"She was late getting home and the children were walking down the road to meet up with her and hurry her along. To do her chores, you know."

"And?" He prompted.

"What? Oh, well, they saw her from the bridge up there," Benjamin pointed toward the side road and the visible, wooden bridge over the creek.

Detective Jones made a mental note to look down on the creek from that vantage point before leaving.

"Her face was in the water," Benjamin added, his voice breaking, So say my daughters.".

"And there was a man standing…., where exactly?" Detective Jones asked, scanning the banks of the creek.

"Uh, Rebecca said he was standing over Suzanna, in the creek, I guess." Benjamin looked at the grassy area between the creek and the county road. "Seems to be a path there, goin' up to the road." He pointed it out.

Detective Jones walked across the creek, looking at the places where the grass had been flattened. It certainly looked like someone had walked up to the road, but there were no tracks. The bank was mostly sand and pebbles and the side of the road was hard-packed dirt. There was a partial tire track, but hardly enough to be considered evidence. He made some notes and walked along the roadway to the intersecting dirt road, turning right to the bridge. He gazed down at the place where the Amish man stood on the sandbar, then beyond him to the clear, running water, close to where they had walked down to the sandy banks earlier.

Benjamin climbed up to the bridge. "Well, what do you think?" He asked.

"Did you find your daughter's *Kapp*?" He asked tenderly.

Benjamin removed his black hat and scratched his hair. "I can't recall," he said, replacing his hat. "Do you need to see it? Maybe my wife has it somewhere."

"Then she was wearing it when she was found?"

"I'm sure she must have been," Benjamin answered. "She's a good, Amish girl. She wouldn't have her *Kapp* off out here in the daylight." He looked up at the younger man. "Is it important?"

"Well, it might be," Detective Jones answered. "There's been some killings around the area and the killer takes Amish *Kapps* as a trophy."

Benjamin frowned, then looked at the other man in disbelief. "What do you mean? Someone is killing Amish women and stealing their *Kapps?* That makes no sense. What would a man want with them?"

"Good question," he answered. "We're still investigating to find the answer to that. However," He stopped walking and turned to look Benjamin full in the face. "This might not be related at all. It would help to know if her *Kapp* is safely at home."

But, it wasn't there. His daughters claimed that it must have floated down the creek because they hadn't seen it at all when they found their sister. Rebecca didn't remember the man having anything in his hands, either. Of course, Martha still claimed she didn't remember a man there at all. Benjamin stated that he did remember her hair hanging over his arm when he carried her home. "I should have noticed it then," he lamented.

It's murder, then, Benjamin said to himself. *Somebody has murdered my oldest girl.* He didn't say anything out loud. He and Detective Jones stared meaningfully at one another, but neither of them spoke to the other. The detective drove away and Benjamin was left to wonder what evil had befallen his daughter, right here in the protective hills of their hollow.

Jeremy drove all night, only stopping to refuel the car and use a restroom. He stuck to Interstate roads into Indiana until he saw a sign that showed pictures of Amish communities. He found an exit and drove to a restaurant to eat some breakfast, using their restroom to wash up. Quite by accident, he saw himself in the full-length mirror on the back of the restroom door. It startled him to see the black circles under his eyes and the red lines around his pupils. He took some energy pills without water and walked to a table to order from the menu. He lingered long over his coffee, listening to the locals talk about the weather, crops, and upcoming births of various animals. At last, out the window, he observed a buggy coming from a road beyond his sight. He quickly paid for his meal so he could drive around town, then out into the country.

"Why do these stupid girls walk around along these country roads?" He asked out loud.

"I suppose you think they're waiting for you," came the snide remark from Dad, again showing up in the rearview mirror.

He smiled. "What are you, jealous?"

Dad laughed. "Hardly, you're just a kid after all. You don't even know how to follow directions yet." There was silence, but Jeremy could still see his father sitting in the back seat, staring at him. "You left a body back there to be found right away. People saw you, talked to you. You sounded pathetic."

"Shut up! Go away! I don't need you!"

To Jeremy's astonishment, Dad was gone, just like that. He smiled as he trolled the back roads of Adams County, Indiana. He finally gave up in the early afternoon to find a motel to stay in. He exercised in the weight room, swam in the pool, and ate a light meal at the café. Then, he went to bed, determined to be successful early the next morning, preferably before full daylight. However, he didn't wake up until well after morning had broken. He was surprised to see that his clock registered 9:42. He stretched, yawning hugely. Putting his hands behind his head, he contemplated what he should do for the day. If he had learned one lesson from the past, it was not to do what he did in the middle of the day. It had to be either early morning or late evening. He had to have time to move the body, too. Dad was right, it was too dangerous to leave them where they fell. He had to be more careful. Jeremy got up and dug out his journal, turning to the page with the map and the plan for this 'finale.' He smiled at his choice of words. He thought about just driving on to Illinois, but his plan said he had to take care of one female in Indiana first, so he had to do what he had to do. "One a day, isn't going to work if I sleep in like this," he mumbled, slowly dragging his fingers through his unruly hair, and closing his journal, his hands caressing the book as though it were a lover. He turned to the bathroom, turned on the shower, and got clean clothes around. "I'll feel better when I've cleaned up and gotten dressed," he said.

Jeremy drove around the county for most of the day, noting creeks and parks, stores and home businesses. He stopped once to fuel up his car and another time to buy some ice cream at a small country store. People in the store looked at him curiously, making him feel like a bug on the wall. Even though he smiled and tried to make small talk, they didn't respond with equal enthusiasm. He began to worry that he might have come here where they knew about him. *They're wary; maybe they know who I am already.* He frowned as he made a turn to drive out into the country, finding a park that offered picnic tables and playground equipment. It was deserted, so he parked and laid himself out on a table near the creek. He must have fallen asleep, because when he opened his eyes it was past sunset. Shadows were gathering amongst the trees nearby. He sat up slowly, stretching his muscles which had cramped from laying on the wooden table.

Kelly often wandered through the park on her way home from her job of cleaning house for an elderly English couple. She loved the time alone, meandering along the creek toward her father's house. She searched for unique shells and rocks to take home to her younger siblings, anticipating their "oohs and ahs" that would greet her as she revealed first one treasure and then another. Sometimes, she would take off her *Kapp* and unwind her hair as she walked through the park. She knew it was a sin, but it felt so good to have the wind blowing through her hair. She always quickly put herself back together before leaving the covering of the trees and brush so that her *Mamm* and *Dat* would never know of her indiscretion. She idly wondered today what Myron would think if he saw her like this. A slow smile crossed her young face. They would marry soon, probably next summer after they both joined church. She envisioned all the preparations to make the house ready for the wedding. Hundreds of people would be invited.

A splash behind her caused her to look back. Her final thought, as she fell to the creek bed, was of Myron....

Jeremy was curious about the Amish girl without her *Kapp*. He calmly walked over to the still form and picked her up. She was slim and tall, he noted. As he laid the body in the trunk of his car, he saw the strings coming out of her apron pocket. He smiled as he pulled out the *Kapp*. "Naughty girl," he whispered. "Already defiant, aren't you?" He closed the trunk, wiped off his bat on the grass, and calmly drove to a state park some miles away to deposit her body in a shallow ravine. He made sure there were no tracks or telltale evidence before driving away. "Next stop, Illinois," he whistled a little tune.

Naomi was no longer young. At 22, she knew she was considered by most to be an *alt maidel* (old maid). "Well, so be it," she said with a stamp of her foot. She knew she was not a pretty girl, too heavy, and not very tall, but so was *Mamm*, and she got a husband. Still, prospects looked bleak. She continued to dust the shelves in the country store where she worked to help pay bills at home. *Dat* broke his back in the spring when he fell from the side of the barn, so she had to help provide for the family. She sighed as she thought of going home to do the chores after working a whole day. *It really isn't fair,* she thought. *I can't very well find a husband when all I get to do is work.*

Duties called as customers began coming into the store and her personal thoughts had to be forsaken for the job at hand. At last, the day was done and she was free to walk the half-mile to her father's home. There was a car in the driveway. She supposed her older brother, John, had come for a visit, as he often did on Wednesdays. He had jumped the fence four years ago when he went to college and got a job in the town of Arthur, as a banker. She wondered why he couldn't have just married Joanne Miller and settled right here in the country with the rest of them. But, he'd married an Englisher who never fit in well with the family, in her opinion, and that's just the way it is.

Before she got up the steps, she could hear raised voices. *On, no!* She thought. *Dat and John must be at it again.* She hesitated before going to the door. *Maybe I should just wait out here for a while, until they have time to work out whatever the problem is this time.* She sat on the top step to look glumly out over the farm. It all looked so calm and serene, but with her father's temper, it was far from it. "John's just as bad," she mumbled under her breath. The side door slammed as John stomped to his car. Never looking back, he revved the engine and spun gravel all over the yard as he sped down the driveway. Naomi watched him speed away before getting up and grabbing a basket to gather vegetables from the garden for supper. *I'll make a good, hearty stew for supper, that's what I'll do!*

It was a quiet supper, her father still fuming from his altercation with her brother. Mam never said much at these times, and everyone else was quiet because of it. She helped red up after dinner and grabbed her shawl. It was time for a walk while Mam and Dat talked over their differences. She knew her mother wanted to still be lenient with her son, but Dat was angry and there would be words yet tonight.

Naomi walked along the dirt road, up a long lane to the small, community pond. There was an old grist mill sitting there along the creek, mostly in ruins now. The stone building was still solid, but all the gears and water wheel, the workings, as Dat would say, was rotting into the ground. Vines and brambles were growing up and over the structure, too. She peeked inside before sitting on an old bench near the water.

"Nice place," said a male voice from across the water.

Naomi was startled and looked up suddenly. A chill passed over her as she realized how very far she was from the protection of her father's house. "It's quiet here," she said shyly, trying to make it less awkward to be talking to a complete stranger, an Englisher at that. She looked around, but saw no car. "How did you get here?" She asked.

He lithely leaped over the creek and came to her, sitting on the grass near her feet. "I left my car over there a ways," he said with a smile.

"Ah," she replied, idly tossing a stick into the rushing water.

"So, you live around here?" He seemed genuinely interested.

"A mile or so over that way," she pointed behind her, down the lane she had just walked. A sudden feeling of vulnerability washed over her, causing her to frown. She stood up and shook some dirt off her apron. "I best be getting back. Dat will be worrying." She felt like running, but didn't know why. The man seemed nice enough, but still, he was a stranger. It didn't seem right. She glanced at him, still sitting there like nothing was wrong, like he talked to strange Amish girls every day. He was caressing a shiny metal bat, balancing it on his hand. He looked up at her and smiled. She smiled back at him as she began walking quickly away. *There's something wrong,* she thought. It was her last thought. As she glanced back again, the bat hit her squarely in the temple and she crumpled to the ground.

Jeremy took his time laying her body in the old mill, arranging her hands across her chest. He took the cap and swung it around and around his hand as he walked calmly back to his car. It was time to move on. He had many miles and 'appointments' to make over the next few days. He felt like whistling, but made not a sound until he was safe in his car, parked in an old sandy pull off near another part of the creek, along the county road. "All you have to do is watch," he mumbled. "These girls are as predictable as the sun rising. They get upset with their folks and go for a walk along a creek somewhere." He made a mark in his journal before driving away. "One more down, one more hat for Mom," he cocked his eyebrow, smiling at the writing on the clean page. Putting the book under his seat, he fastened his seat belt and drove away. He was many miles away when Naomi was found by a search party her father had gathered. He never knew of any of the families and lives he affected with his deeds. He truly didn't care. He now had a goal, and a plan to get there. All was well.

Jeremy drove through the night into Missouri. He stopped at a small motel early in the morning and slept away the daylight hours. He didn't feel hungry, just incredibly tired. When he awoke at last, the sun was waning in the west, shining through his window. He didn't remember there being a window when he checked in and hadn't closed the drapes.

"You're getting sloppy," Dad said from the end of the bed.

"Shut up," Jeremy mumbled. "Why won't you leave me alone?"

Dad laughed, a sound that was eerily like his own laughter. *When was the last time I laughed at anything?* Jeremy wondered idly. *When was the last time I golfed or played racquetball?* He shook his head to rid his mind of these useless thoughts. "I have a mission," he said aloud.

"Right," Dad sneered.

Jeremy looked at the man clearly sitting on the bed beside his feet. "Why?" He pled.

"After all this time, you still don't know why?"

Jeremy shook his head as he sat up, raising his knees near his chest. "When did this begin? I know what the end has to be, but…" He stopped suddenly and looked again at the figure sitting so close to him. "Get away from me!" He yelled, wrapping his arms around his head as he leaned into his knees. "Just go away and leave me alone!" Jeremy fell back into his pile of pillows, sobbing, rocking his upper torso back and forth across the bed. At last, he calmed and stopped crying. He reached for his phone to dial the familiar number.

"Hello?" Came his mother's plaintive, rather whiney voice.

"It's me, Mom," Jeremy replied. "Just wanted to hear your voice."

"Oh, Jeremy," she breathed into the phone. "Are you nearby, Honey? Are you going to come home?"

"No, I'm…I'm out working. I just needed to hear you. Are you and Grandma okay?"

"Of course we are," she replied. "We're worried about you, though."

"No need."

"Please come home now, Jeremy," she pleaded.

"I'll be there soon enough," He mumbled. "Mom?"

"Yes?"

"What's wrong with me?"

"What do you mean? What's going on, Jerr?"

"Did you ever think there was something wrong with me? I mean, we went to that counselling when I was a kid and all,"

"Well, you had seen your father die, Jeremy, when you were very young. I thought it might have affected you somehow. And with Jack leaving like he did, too, well, you know, I did my best for you."

There was an awkward silence while he processed what she had just said. *She didn't admit to killing Dad or Jack, and she didn't deny it, either,* he thought. A deep sigh escaped him.

"Jeremy, come home. We can go to counseling again; together, if you need to."

"Heh," he answered. "It's a little late for that now, don't you think, Mom?"

"What do you mean? It's never too late to get help."

"I gotta go, gotta get some stuff done," he said before clicking the off button.

The Unravelling

The phone was ringing as Anna rushed into the house, arms full of groceries. She reached for the phone, but knocked it to the floor in her hurry. She set the bags on the counter and ran to retrieve the receiver from the floor. "Hello?" She said breathlessly.

"Anna?" She recognized her mother's voice.

"Yes, Mom, it's me."

"Is something wrong?"

"No, no," Anna waved her free hand. "I was just coming in with some bags of food and hit the phone. What's up?"

"Have you heard from Jeremy lately?"

"Not for about a week or so, but that's not unusual." Her brow creased with worry lines. "Why, is something wrong?"

"Oh, I'm not sure, just wondering where he is these days."

"Well, you know him. He's travelling around making sales." She paused a few seconds. "Who would have thought he would be such a successful real estate broker?"

"Yes," now her mother paused. "Say, Anna, has he brought you any more of those Amish hats?"

Anna smiled through her chuckle. "Yes, why? Do you want one, too?"

"No!" Her mother said quickly. "Um, no, I was just wondering if he was making that a hobby or pattern, or something."

"What're you getting at, Mom?"

There was a long pause.

"Mom? Are you still on the line?"

"Yes, well, Anna, do you watch the news?"

Anna frowned, taking the receiver from her ear to look at it as though it might reveal something she hadn't heard. "Um, not very often. Boring and depressing stuff, the news." She had to repress a another giggle.

"Yes, well you know I went to the editor's conference recently…"

"How'd that go?"

"What? Oh, it was fine, just fine." There was another pause. "The other night, there was a story about an Amish girl who was killed. Tragic story, but the worst part of it is…I learned this at the conference…there's been more than one of these deaths of young Amish girls."

"And this has you in a dither?" Anna began putting groceries away, lifting the long phone cord over the counter to do so.

"Well, tell me, where has Jeremy brought those hats from lately?"

"What?" She stopped what she was doing and looked out the kitchen window. She could see the little copse of trees where Jeremy spent so much time as a boy.

"I don't know, Mom. They're all different, you know. So, I guess he's trying to send me a collection or something, one from each state he goes to, I think."

"What states, Anna?" Mom's voice was filled with emotion, but Anna couldn't decipher the cause.

"Well, Pennsylvania, of course, but you knew about that one. Then, I think maybe Missouri, perhaps Indiana. Like I said, I don't really know." She paused. "I thought I would label them some time, but I haven't done it. Actually, he has sent little notes about which states. I hope I've saved those so I can label the hats."

"Anna!" Her mother said sharply. "Pay attention! You're so scattered." Jean Brown, her mother, now sounded cross.

"I'm scattered? Mom, you've been talking in circles for at least ten minutes. What is going on?"

"Listen to me. Three Amish girls have been found and one is missing in Indiana. The others are from Pennsylvania, Tennessee, and Missouri. Doesn't that seem a bit odd to you?"

"I guess it is odd that there are missing and dead Amish girls, but I don't get what you're thinking, Mom." A sudden fear passed over Anna's body. She almost couldn't speak the feeling was so strong. "Surely you are not suggesting that Jeremy had anything to do with this?"

"I don't know, Anna. I don't believe in coincidences, and this seems too odd to be unconnected." She paused to let Anna speak, but when there was no more conversation, she continued. "When you and Jeremy were getting counseling, did he ever talk about his dad? Did you ever talk to him about Jack?"

"What?" Anna said. "Mom, they don't tell you what your kid said in a counseling session. This line of conversation is making me mad. What has any of this got to do with Jeremy? This is OUR Jeremy we're talking about, you know."

"I do know," Jean almost whispered.

"I don't know if he talked about his dad's death much or not. He's never talked to me about it, or about Jack leaving, either." She paused in thought. "You know, Ken, his counselor, did talk to me about something Jerr said, hmm, something he was mixing up about Charlie and Jack's deaths. Not that Jack is dead, but you know what I mean. It wasn't serious though, I don't think, 'cause he said he thought Jerr was getting better at that time."

"I see," Jean said quietly.

"Mom, surely you don't think Jeremy is a killer, a serial killer, for God's sake!" She took the phone from her ear and shook it in the air. Tears welled up before spilling down her face.

"Anna, I'm just saying all of this is very odd. I don't know, maybe my imagination is getting the best of me, but I keep feeling there could be a connection." No response from Anna. "Where is he now?"

"Ohio or Kentucky, I think. There! He's not in Indiana, so your connection is broken. And so is this one." She hung the phone angrily on the wall. "How dare she!" She yelled into the silent room. She slid down the wall to the floor, sobs coming in great gulps as she fought to control the anger and fear that assailed her. When the phone began ringing again, she laid back on the floor and ignored it. "I can't do this right now," she whispered, clasping her hands over her ears until the incessant ringing stopped. "I won't listen to any more of this."

The phone rang every hour, but Anna refused to answer. When the doorbell rang, she hid in her bedroom, covering her head with a pillow. But, that didn't help. Jean had a key. In moments, she was shaking her daughter. "Anna, I don't mean to upset you, but…"

"There is no but, Mom, you are upsetting me!" Anna flung the pillow away from her and sat up, moving away from her mother. "Don't touch me," she spat out.

"Anna..."

"No!" Anna raised her hand to stop the words. "No, I won't listen to such diatribe!"

"I know it's difficult to hear..."

"No! No, you don't!"

"Anna..."

"Stop! I won't hear it, I tell you, I won't!"

"Why? Because you know it isn't true or because you fear it could be?" Jean said gently.

"Are you crazy? How can you even connect Jeremy to this?"

"I don't want to, Anna, but let's go over the facts, okay?"

"There aren't any facts, Mom. You have taken some kind of story and put it on Jeremy because you know he got mental help as a teen."

Jean looked sadly at her daughter. "You know that isn't true."

"Well, what else could it possibly be?"

"It could be that there is more going on with this man than we know."

Anna frowned. "What man?"

"Jeremy, of course. He's not a boy any more, Anna. He's a man, grown up, out on his own."

Anna shook her head. "I know, but he'll always be my boy."

"Yes, of course, in one way that's true. But, he's a man, nonetheless, and we have to face the fact that he has a life we don't really know about. That's what happens. Our children grow up and do things they don't tell us about, because they don't have to anymore, after all."

Anna waved her mother away. "I know this, Mother."

"Jeremy had some problems in his youth..."

"See? There you go, labelling him."

Mom looked sternly at her daughter. "Anna, please just listen. Schizophrenia is hereditary. Whatever is happening to him may not be entirely his fault if he is having some kind of fantasy, paranoia, or delusions or something."

"I don't want to listen to this. It doesn't make any sense to me." With that, she got up and fled to the kitchen where she began unpacking the groceries all over again, this time actually putting them away. She was aware of her mother standing near the counter watching her.

"Their *Kapps* were missing, Anna. All of the dead Amish girls had missing *Kapps*."

"And that's enough to accuse your grandson of murder?" Anna stood with her hands on her hips, a loaf of bread dangling at her side. Her face was red with anger.

"Doesn't that seem odd to you, in the least bit?"

"No, it does not." She continued putting away her food before sitting on a stool at the counter.

Jean had moved to the window, looking out into the back yard. "Anna, what is that little rock shrine out there in the trees?"

"I don't know for sure," she said quietly. "He built it so long ago, just after Jack left."

"Remember when he used to kill cats…"

"And squirrels and rabbits, Mom. He's a boy. He's put plenty of food on our table." She paused. "I kind of miss that." There was a moment of silence. "His counselor knew about that, too. We talked about it, about Jeremy killing animals. He didn't seem too worried."

"What did he do with the dead cats?"

"He buried them, I think," Anna shrugged. "Funny thing…" She stopped, putting her elbows on the counter, her fingers covering her mouth.

"What is it, Honey?" Mom looked so worried.

"He only killed female cats. He said they produced too many babies."

They stared into one another's eyes for several moments.

"How strange," Mom muttered. Slowly, she turned from the window. "How did he kill all these animals?"

Anna smiled with some disdain. "Remember that little metal bat he got? He practiced on a target behind the garage for days on end. Then, he began bringing down bats and birds and squirrels, and of course, the cats."

"I don't understand," Mom frowned.

"Well, he got so good at it, he could hit them square in the head with one swing. It was rather amazing to watch." Anna looked up, uncertainty clouding her face. "He did have to hit them again sometimes, but not very often. He's really good with that bat. It kind of imbeds in the skull of those little animals." A shudder passed over her body.

"Oh, Anna," Mom breathed. "These girls had a crushed skull at the temple, an indentation, or hole. Every one of them. Evidently, they died instantly. Police are still trying to discover the murder weapon." She paused in thought. "Where's the bat now?"

Anna bowed her head down to the counter, putting her hands over her ears. She shook her head from side to side as though trying to erase the memory of what was just said.

"Was the neighbor's dog ever found?" Mom persisted.

"No," Anna said into her chest, muffling the sound of her voice.

"I'm willing to bet; I could be wrong…but I would wager that the remains of that dog are under the shrine."

"I repeat, are you crazy?" Anna lifted her head, her eyes bloodshot with unshed tears.

"Let's dig it up. I'll prove that much to you, and then you must face these other facts."

"I will not!" Anna stretched her neck, rubbing the back of her head. "Mom, you're giving me a headache. Please go home and write a book or something. This story is too bizarre for me."

"If I go out there and dig that up, and the bones are there, will you believe me?"

"Why would I even let you do that?"

"Because you want to know as much as I do. Anna," her mother sat next to her for a moment, laying a gentle hand on her daughter's shoulder. "We cannot let this go on. If we know something about this, we must let the authorities know."

"The auth… Mom, you're talking about Jeremy!"

"I know." She waited a moment. "He's got the bat with him, doesn't he?" Jean whispered.

Suddenly, Anna got up from her chair and walked to the garage door. "Come on, let's get this over with. I will prove to you, that this is not even a possibility." She threw open the door, reaching for the garden spade hanging on the wall. "Jeremy did not kill that dog and he is not a killer now."

"Good!" Jean retorted. "Let's do that."

An hour later, they stood looking down at the bones of a small dog, buried deep under the rock in the trees. Anna stood staring in disbelief. "It can't be," she whispered. They also unearthed a kitchen knife in the dirt, the blade rusted from being out in the elements, the remains of a plastic bag showing that he had tried to preserve it. "I wondered what happened to this knife from my set in the kitchen…" Her voice trailed off into a smothered sob.

"I'm sorry, Honey," Jean soothed. "Look at the head. It's smashed to bits, fractures and downright breaks. He must have beat it in the head over and over."

"This doesn't mean he's killed any people." Anna defended her son.

"True, but the likelihood of it is high."

"Don't talk to me!" Anna threw down her shovel and stomped to the house.

Jean looked at the collar to verify the dog's ownership, then silently shoveled the dirt back into the hole. She didn't bother to put the stone back, just took the shovel and put it in the garage, slipped the knife into a box on the work bench, then let herself into the house.

Anna was upstairs in Jeremy's room looking through his things, left there when he moved out. There were comic books and GI Joe figures, a few clothes, a bowling ball in the bag with his shoes, and posters on his walls, posters of trees, of flowers, but no sports teams or bands, things other teens might have. Everything was neat as usual. Except for there being so few clothes, it was as if he never left.

"What are you looking for?"

"I don't know." Anna sat on the floor, her eyes dry, but a sorrowful look filling her face and eyes.

"Let's take it one step at a time. We have to be sure, can't just have no evidence at all."

Anna got up and walked into her bedroom where she had three Amish *Kapps* on a shelf against the wall above her dresser. She grabbed them off the shelf and threw them onto the bed. "We have these," she squeaked. "Is that evidence enough?"

"Is the bat in his room?"

Anna sadly shook her head, staring at the head coverings strewn on her bed. "Take a look in the back of his closet," she whispered.

Jean walked back to Jeremy's room, opened the closet and peered deep into it. There was a pillow and blanket, a water bottle, and a book of some kind.

"Where is he, Anna?" she asked when she returned to her daughter's room

"I don't know for sure. He only calls once or twice a month." She heaved a big sigh. "I know he isn't home, because I called the lady who cleans the house for him. Surely, she would notice if there was something so bizarre as you are describing. It can't be Jeremy, Mom! It can't be!"

"Jeremy left a mess? That's hard to believe." She poked her head into his room and looked around. "He cleaned this, right? I mean, he always cleans up after himself, that I know of."

Anna looked at her mother as though she was seeing her for the first time. "You're right; it is odd, but she said he left dirty dishes in the sink and some laundry undone." She paused. "One other time, I remember he left his cereal bowl in the sink, cereal and all. He'd tried to clean up the table, but didn't get everything. When I asked him about it, he said he'd heard something that scared him so he just threw the stuff in the sink and went to school. That's been so long ago, I'd almost forgotten."

The doorbell rang, startling them both, and causing Anna to go to the window. "UPS," she said over her shoulder.

"Are you expecting something?"

"No, but sometimes Jerr…" she turned quickly, nearly running down the stairs, jerked open the front door and brought the package into the kitchen. She used a knife to open the lid.

"Who's it from?" Jean asked.

"It's from him, from Ohio," she added, tapping the label on the box.

Slowly, she drew out two Amish *Kapps*. They hung from her fingers, two head coverings of different styles. Anna reached into the box for the envelope with her name on it. '*To Mom*,' it said. Her hands began shaking as she opened the envelope. She shoved the letter toward her mother. "I can't read this right now."

"Do you want me to read it aloud?"

Anna nodded.

"*Mom.*

Here's the latest for your collection of hats. Why did you start this? It's too hard, Mom. But, Dad is with me most days and that makes it easier because he understands your plan. I don't know what happened to Jack. Don't tell me, though. I don't want to know. Anyway, I'm on my way to Kentucky and then back out to Illinois before making a trip clear up to Wisconsin, maybe. I love being able to travel and see so many natural wonders.

BTW: these are from Indiana and Ohio. Made a sale in Ohio, but picked up the other hat on my way through Indiana. No sales there. I have two possible sales in Illinois, so I might be gone longer than usual.

Jeremy

"What does he mean by 'why did you start this' and 'your plan?' Mom asked with a frown.

"I don't know. The first *Kapp* he brought me, he said was for a collection and alluded to Jack's ball cap and his dad's fishing hat as a part of my collection of hats."

"You kept Charlie's fishing hat?"

"It was hanging in the closet and I put it up in the garage. It's still there, I guess. I haven't moved it."

Her mother got up and looked in the garage. "Yep, it's there."

"Really, Mom, I don't care if it is or isn't."

"He always cuts one of the strings off, doesn't he?" Jean asked, holding up the pair of head coverings.

"Does he? Maybe they sell them that way, or something. Isn't that what we decided a long time ago? He buys these things and they are imperfect so no one can wear them?"

"Maybe," her mother agreed. "But, look at the cuts, Anna. It looks like someone just cut off one of them below the stitching." *And maybe he has his own collection,* Jean thought. "Well, whatever he does, he thinks you are driving this train of horror. I'm no psychiatrist, but I believe he thinks you killed Charlie and Jack, and for some reason he has to kill to..."

Anna looked at her mother in horror. "To what? I didn't kill anyone! If I could have gotten to Charlie faster, I would have stopped him." She hung her head. "But, I didn't, he slit his throat like it was easy, or something." Her voice had become a whisper.

"And Jeremy saw that happen. He was only three, so who knows what he thought, what he put together?"

"I know. I'm a terrible mother."

"Oh, Honey. I don't think that. You shouldn't either. Charlie had so many problems. You probably couldn't have stopped him even if you tried. He might even have killed you, too." She hurried on with the thought. "By accident, I mean."

"I should've sat that boy down and explained it all to him when he said there was blood under the desk," Anna waved her hand toward the desk in the dining room. "I should've made sure he understood that his father had a mental disorder that distorted all of his beliefs and emotions. I should've held him more as he was growing up, and made sure he knew what happened."

"You were in shock and grief yourself, Dear." Jean soothed. "This isn't your fault."

"It's no excuse for not following through with my son." She looked up at her mother with horror in her eyes. "Have I made this monster? Is he a monster?"

"Oh, my, no," Jean pulled her daughter into a tight hug. "This isn't your fault. We don't even know if there's something to worry about. Maybe I've made too much of a news story and there's no connection at all."

Anna pulled back. "And put me through this for fun?" Her voice took on a tenor of anger.

"No, of course not. I just meant that to soothe you. Please don't blame yourself. We aren't sure of anything, yet."

"Aren't we?" Anna whimpered, laying her head on her mother's shoulder. They stood that way for several minutes, until Anna stopped shuddering, trying to control her sobs.

"As I said earlier, one thing at a time." Jean said. "Let me do some investigating into this story and either match up facts or find fault that gives us reasonable doubt, okay?"

"No police?" Anna hiccupped.

"Not yet," Jean smiled, patting her daughter's hair back out of her face. "Do you want me to stay the night?" She asked.

Anna nodded. "That would be nice. I sure don't want to be alone."

Do you have a key to Jeremy's house, then?"

"Yes," Anna whispered. "I thought, too, that we should go there and search for it; the bat, I mean." She paused. "We know he isn't home and he trusts me to go there." Another sob rose and choked her.

"Let's go tomorrow, then. I think we need to rest, tonight, and it's a long drive." Jean said as she patted Anna's back.

"I'm not going to sleep." Anna said with a shake of her head.

"I know, that's why I said let's get some rest."

Jean made them some peppermint tea to help her daughter remain calm. Methodically, they cleaned up the kitchen, then sat in the living room near the gas fireplace. Jean lit the fire, not bothering to turn on any lights. Eventually Anna did go to sleep, curled up on the couch. Jean quietly went into the kitchen where she called a friend, a detective she knew really well. "James, I need to be able to tell you a horror story and trust you'll help me out here," she said by way of introduction to her topic.

"Well, that sounds ominous," Detective Conrad commented. "What's going on?"

"Have you heard about the Amish girls that have been killed recently, that is, over the past three or four years? All over the place, not just here in Ohio."

"You talking about the missing head coverings that's begun to look like a link in several states?" James asked. He sat up at his desk and began making notes. "What do you know about it?"

"Maybe nothing," she answered. "That's why I called you personally. This needs kid gloves and care so we don't make a mistake. Maybe I'm thinking overtime."

"Go on, Jean, but I have to tell you that I'm making notes. If we discover this really is something, I'll need them."

"I understand," she said. "You know my grandson, Jeremy…" she began.

"Sure, nice kid," he responded. "Quiet type, never in any trouble."

"Hmmm, yes, well, he's a real estate broker, nationally. He travels all over the place, selling properties no one else can sell, or something like that." Pleasure crept into her voice, to be able to brag about her only grandson. "He's very successful."

James Conrad frowned, his piercing blue eyes focused on the legal pad he was about to write on. A lock of his blond hair fell onto his forehead which he pushed back by habit.

Jean continued. "He's been sending his mother Amish *Kapps* from the states he visits because he thinks she wants to collect them." Jean sighed. She wasn't sure she could go on with this. It was beginning to sound crazy to her own ears.

"And you think, well, tell me what you think about this, Jean. Take your time. I can hear the emotion in your voice."

"Oh, James, I think he might be killing those girls!" She blurted out with a sob. "I don't have any proof, just the *Kapps*, and he has that little bat; oh, my, I don't know what to think."

"How did you find out about this case? It's still in the investigation stage." He countered.

"I went to an editor's conference in Cincy last week. Someone was talking about it there, trying to connect dots. I listened, then just began putting two and two together. Please tell me I am coming up with five, not four."

"Let's get together tomorrow and take a look at the facts, Jean. I'd like to see these *Kapps*, too. Have you been handling them?"

"My daughter has. I hope we haven't compromised any evidence. I didn't even think there could be DNA there. Oh, my, what have we done?"

"It's okay. I'll take it from here. Can I come over to your place in the morning?"

"I'm at Anna's. She doesn't know I've called you." Jean took a breath. "She's in denial, of course, but she'll come around. There's so much more to the story, James."

"There usually is." He paused. "You said something about a bat. Got time to elaborate on that a little?"

"Yes, when he was twelve or thirteen, I guess, Anna bought him a metal, mini baseball bat. Evidently, he is really, really good at killing small animals with it. You know, squirrels and rabbits. He's also killed cats, a lot of neighborhood cats, I believe." She paused. "Anna says he can kill them with one hit of the bat, by throwing it, imbedding it into their heads," she sniffled, trying to stifle her desire to sob openly.

James whistled, raking his fingers through his wavy hair again. "Jean, I don't know what to say right now. I'll get up to speed tonight, though. Get some rest now, and I'll come over in the morning. I'll take all the blame for our interlude."

They rang off and Jean idly walked around the house. She checked on Anna, covering her with an afghan from the back of the couch. Street lights illuminated the front of the house, giving an eerie glow to the yard, the shadows made by trees and buildings taking on a sinister feel. "I am scared to death for my own grandson," she muttered. "Oh, Jeremy, what are you doing?"

Probing Life

Anna sat uncomfortably on her own couch. "Why'd you invite this guy over?" She asked her mother.

"We have to face some facts and find out what is, or is not, going on," Jean said quietly, handing her daughter a cup of mint tea. "This will calm you."

"I doubt it, but it is your answer to everything," Anna said, taking a sip. "When will he be here?"

Jean shrugged. "He said this morning, so anytime, I guess."

"I'm not sure what there is to talk about. We're, that is, you are doing a lot of guesswork because of some coincidences with Jeremy; some stuff he did as a kid. I don't see the connection." She looked steadfastly at her cup.

Jean smiled. "Yes, you do. Don't try to fool me. You're as concerned about this as I am." She heaved a sigh. "Let's not pretend we don't know what we know."

"What you seem to know," Anna persisted. "I can still see him, sitting right here," she patted the cushion beside her, "doing his homework, innocent as all get out."

Jean frowned at her daughter, her only child. "That's been years ago, Anna. Jeremy is a man, now. And if we're right, he's a very sick man who needs to be stopped before there can be any more killing."

Anna looked up, her face stricken with fear and a little anger. "How can you say that so easily about Jeremy?" She gave a sigh, "It can't be true, not my boy, not Jeremy."

"Let's gather the facts and follow them to the truth. If I'm wrong, I'll be the first to admit it. He'll never know from my lips that I considered him for this, okay?"

Anna nodded.

The doorbell rang through the house, jangling both their nerves. "He must be here," Anna whispered.

"I'll get it," Jean announced as she rose from her seat. When she got to the door, she was surprised by the waving UPS driver, heading back to his truck. A box was set neatly beside the door. "Oh, no," she breathed. She reached down for the box as a car pulled into the driveway. She was relieved to see James get out of his car and saunter up to her.

"Good morning, Jean," he smiled.

Jean woodenly smiled back, the box held gingerly in her hands. "Hello, James," she said weakly. "Come on in." She held open the door.

"What's wrong?" He asked, a look of concern on his face.

Jean held up the box as she led the way into the living room. Anna was not on the couch, indeed, not even in the room. "Now what," Jean breathed.

Anna made an entrance into the room, wearing a flowered dress and pumps. She looked fresh and happy. "Hello," she offered a hand to James.

Jean frowned at her. "What are you doing?" She hissed.

Anna waved her mother away as she graciously offered their guest a seat. She looked back at her mother, noticing the box for the first time. "What's that?" She frowned.

"Another box from Jeremy," Jean said, handing it to Anna. "From Tennesee."

Anna turned pale, placing the box on the floor next to her feet.

"Aren't you going to open it?" Jean asked.

"Not now, Mom." Anna shook her head.

James watched the interaction between the two women. *There really may be something here,* he thought for the first time. He observed his hostesses. He'd known Jean for a number of years, but not on a personal level. He'd met Anna once or twice at ball games or at the school. This was the first close encounter he'd had with either of them, and it wouldn't be easy from what he could see of their nervousness. *Treat it like any other investigation,* he told himself. *She's a beautiful woman,* he admired Anna.

Shaking his head slightly, he reminded himself, *this is just another case. No personal involvement, that's the policy.*

He cleared his throat. "I, uh, took the liberty of talking to a few people about your, uh, Jeremy." He began.

"What do you mean? Who?" Anna was angered by this invasion of her son's life. In an aside to her mother, she gave a snarling whisper. "I thought we agreed, no cops yet!"

"Well, I spoke to some of his teachers, his coach, an employer, and uh, his step-dad, Jack, er Jackie."

"You just went ahead and contacted people before even talking to us?" Anna accused, looking meanly at her mother.

"I did," he admitted. "It's what I would do for background in any case."

"Any case?" Anna sat upright, clearly offended. "So, all of a sudden, we're a case?"

"Anna, it's his job," Jean laid a hand on her daughter's arm. "This is what we need to do to either clear him or..." she couldn't finish.

Anna looked at her mother in horror, drawing her shoulder away. "This is not what I expected," she sobbed, hiding her face in a pillow.

"Of course not," her mother soothed, rubbing her back.

"Don't touch me!" Anna's voice was muffled by the pillow. She moved to the floor, knocking over the box. She moved away from it as though it were on fire, sitting glumly on the floor near a chair, pillow clutched in her lap.

"Clearly, this is difficult," James began.

"Don't talk to me," Anna spat out. She turned her head toward the picture window.

"It's okay," Jean assured him. "What did you find out?"

James shrugged. "Basically, that Jeremy was well liked. He had some problems when he was about ten, but got through that period. A Mrs. Williams was watchful of him, worried, then felt he pulled through it." He paused for any comments from the women. When there was nothing, he resumed. "Jackie thought a lot of the boy and was saddened when he and his lifestyle change were discovered by Jeremy. He said you never told the boy the truth, that you let him think Jack had died." He directed his gaze at Anna

Anna nodded, "Yes, I did that. It was so much easier to let him believe that than to try to explain what really happened. I didn't know how to tell a ten-year old that his beloved step-father decided to become a woman and leave us in the dust; then he got older and it didn't seem necessary."

"But, he found out anyway," Jean put in. "By chance, he saw Jack in his, or rather, her new identity." Anna nodded forlornly.

James whistled. "That had to be tough."

"But, it wasn't," Anna spoke up. "It was as though he absorbed the information and needed no explanation or anything." There was a rather awkward silence as James made notes. "And then, as I said, he grew up and didn't seem to need details."

"There was that one note," Jean added. "The one where he said he 'didn't want to know' about Jack." Anna nodded in agreement. "It was after the killings started…"

James indicated the box on the floor, near Anna's feet. "Is that a new hat?"

Anna looked at the box, but made no move to touch it. She shook her head. "I don't know," she whispered, dread filling her face, tears running down her cheeks and dripping from her chin.

"We should look, Dear," Jean said gently. "So, James can investigate, if necessary."

Anna struggled to open the box, but finally pulled back the flaps, pulled out the paper stuffing, and peered inside. What she saw, was a shock. There was not an Amish *Kapp,* but a leather tam, one that was worn and rather dirty. "What on earth?" She breathed.

They all stared in disbelief. "Any note?" Jean asked.

Anna looked inside the box, almost missing the hand-written note laying in the bottom of the box. "It says, 'Greetings from Kentucky. Surprise!" A sob left her mouth as she raised her hand to touch her lips.

James opened a plastic evidence bag which held it out to her. "Just put it in here," he advised.

Woodenly, Anna dropped the hat into the bag, then covered her face with her hands. "What does this mean?" She cried in anguish.

"I'm not sure," James said quietly. "I'll contact someone in Kentucky and see if there's any connection to what we're looking at."

"Thank you, James," Jean nodded as she enveloped her daughter in her arms. They sat together on the floor, holding one another.

James took his leave of them, still missing a lot of information, but interested now in the new hat and what it might tell him. "So, I'm not looking for an Amish girl this time," he muttered as he drove away.

To his dismay, there was no murder report that matched the ones he already had in his file. No John or Jane Doe bodies fit the description of what happened to the Amish girls, not indented skulls where a small bat might have been used. He sat back in his chair and ran a hand over his face. "Maybe this is all a coincidence, after all," he spoke to the paperwork on his desk.

About a week later, he received a Missing Person of Interest Report from Kentucky. It seems a young girl who had frequented a small town had disappeared. The girl was an orphan, as far as anyone knew, a restless teenager who sometimes worked in the local restaurant or the gas station for spending money. She hadn't been seen for several weeks and had left her belongings, meager, but hers, nonetheless, at a rooming house where she stayed, paying her rent by cleaning and running errands. In a few days, he received another report. The girl had been found by hunters at an abandoned mine site, a sizable wound in the side of her head.

"It is him," James breathed out into his empty office.

The Killing Continues

Jeremy couldn't sleep. He tossed and turned for a while, until he got twisted up in his sheet. Kicking his way out of the bed, he stumbled to the window where he looked down on his car across the parking lot from his motel room. Torrential rain fell, rushing across the glass and distorting his view of the car. It looked like…"What does that look like?" He mumbled. He imagined a large turtle which quickly blossomed in his mind to a dragon, a fire-breathing dragon that was held at bay by the water building up in pools in the parking lot. He shook his head firmly. "Foolishness," he said. He looked back at the bed, but it wasn't inviting. The clock on the night stand burned bright red, registering 3:32. Jeremy raised his hands up and stretched, yawning loudly. He ran his fingers through his hair before dropping them to his side. When he turned back to the window, he was astonished to see the little girl, Meghan, from Kentucky looking back at him. He stepped back, gasping at the apparition. "What?" He frowned, peering out into the rain-drenched world. "It can't be," he whispered, rubbing furiously at his eyes. She was standing next to his car, lounging against the front fender, her clothes soaked through, as though she hadn't a care in the world. She gazed steadily up at him, then smiled before vanishing altogether.

Jeremy sank down to his knees, resting his head on his hands upon the windowsill. He realized he was breathing in gulps, yet very shallow, almost like he couldn't get a good breath at all. He turned, sitting down along the wall to rest his butt on the carpeted floor. He held his hands over his eyes, palms pushing against his face. As his breathing calmed, he lowered his hands, resting his forearms against his knees, his hands dangling, head still lowered.

How long he sat that way, he had no idea. He might even have fallen asleep, but what he did know is that light was streaming through the window when he regained true consciousness. Timidly, he got onto his knees again and peered over the sill. His car sat in a puddle of water, the sunshine causing it to shine into his eyes. He breathed a sigh; there was no apparition.

He slowly got to his feet, stretching his kinked muscles. "Whew! Man, you need a shower! He exclaimed into the room. He got some clothes out of the dresser where they were arranged neatly into piles, and went into the bathroom, shutting the door firmly behind him, then just stood there looking at it before locking it.

When he came out, he was only a little surprised to see his father sitting on the bed. But, he was totally shocked to see the girl. *What was her name? Meghan, that's right.* He stared in disbelief. "What, er what's she doing here?" He croaked.

"Who?" Dad said, looking around.

"Come on, Dad, no games. There's a girl sitting right beside you. Meghan, or something," his voice broke as he spoke.

Dad got up and walked toward him, stopping like always, a couple of armlengths away. "You're seeing things, Boy. Calm down. We don't want no women here, now, do we?"

Jeremy stared at his father, then looked around him at the now empty bed. He rubbed his head and went to the mirror. Even the vision of his father disappeared as he looked into the glass. He turned around and surveyed the room, running his hands through his still-damp hair. "You're right about one thing," he said. "I am in panic mode and need to do something to calm down. This is out of hand." He suddenly thought of the counselor he talked to as a teen. "I wonder what happened to him?" He whispered. "Maybe…"

Shaking himself, he began to pack up his clothes. He flung everything into his bag and went to check out, picking up the bill from the floor in front of the door on his way out. After he settled up at the desk, he walked out into the sunshine, stepping carefully around and between puddles on his way to the car. Once inside, he felt safe again. He settled into the driver's seat, hands firmly on the steering wheel.

"What are you doing?" Dad asked.

Jeremy looked into his rearview mirror, relieved that only the road behind him was in his line of vision. "Well, we shall see what we shall see," he replied. A crooked smile spread across his mouth, but his eyes remained focused on the road. "Yes, just you wait and see what's next, Old Man."

There was no response which caused Jeremy to laugh out loud. Things had changed there in that motel room. "Yes, indeedy," he said aloud. "Who just grew up and got control of this situation?" He paused, looking at each of the mirrors. "Now, you will all see what's important and how to accomplish this work." He drove down the road, into rural Tennessee, whistling a happy toon.

Puzzle Pieces

"Jack," Anna said into the phone. "I really need to talk to you. Please call me back. It's about Jeremy and it's rather urgent." She paused, "Sorry, it's still hard for me to call you Jackie. Please, please call me." She hung up the phone on the kitchen wall and walked into the living room. The empty box from Jeremy still lay on its side on the carpet. Idly, she picked It up. As she walked to the garage, she began methodically tearing it into pieces. She noticed one place where a postmark showed it had been mailed from Knoxville, TN. She laid that piece on the desk and put the rest of the box into the trash can in the garage.

She got out some cleaning supplies and began cleaning out the refrigerator. There really wasn't much to do, but she needed to keep busy. Finally, the phone rang and she ran to answer it, dropping her sponge into the bowl of water.

"Hello?" She breathed.

"Anna? Is that you?" Jackie asked.

"Yes, thank you for calling back."

"What's going on? Is Jeremy okay? There hasn't been an accident or something, has there?"

"What?" She frowned at the question. "Oh, no, no, nothing like that." Tears spilled down her cheeks. "Oh, Jack, I don't know where to begin," a sob escaped her.

"Hey, take it easy," Jackie crooned. "It can't be that bad, right? Just start at the beginning. What did the kid do anyway?"

"He's hardly a kid anymore, you know," she said, gaining control of herself.

"Well, I guess that's true."

"Anyway, the police are investigating some killings and, and..."

"Some what?" There was a pause. "Are you out of your mind?"

"Please listen," she begged. "Jeremy may be involved in some killings. We're still not sure what's going on, but he's doing some very strange things, and sending the hats to me, and stuff. There's all those Amish girls who were killed, and he's been at every place. He used to kill the neighborhood cats with that stupid bat, and now he may be doing this, too. Even Mom believes it could be him. Oh, Jack, I don't know what to do!"

"Will you slow down? How did he even get involved? What does that mean, anyway? You haven't made sense for the past ten minutes!"

"I know," she whimpered. "I know. I'm sorry I bothered you with this. Don't worry, we'll get through it to the truth somehow. I'm sorry..." She hung up the phone. Within a minute, it rang again, but she didn't answer it. "It was a mistake. I'm sorry," she muttered to the phone on the wall, fleeing to her bedroom.

"Damn!" Jackie cursed at the phone. "She won't answer the phone now." Jackie walked to the window and looked out into yet another perfectly sunny day in Southern California. "Maybe I should go out there and see what's going on." There was a pause in her thoughts as she stared at palm trees swaying in the breeze. "First, that cop calls me to talk about Jeremy, then Anna starts talking crazy." Jackie imagined what the response would be if she were to return to her old home town. "I just can't go back." Tears ran unbidden down her face. "What's happened to my little boy?" An image of a youth on a bicycle starring at her in the yellow Jeep flashed through her mind. He wasn't a kid even then, she remembered how grownup looking he had appeared, even with the bicycle. "Good Lord, by now he's twenty; a man!" She shook her head slowly as she ran her hands up the back of her head, raking her fingers through the soft curls. "Still, killing someone? I can't believe that." Jackie got out her phone and looked up the number that was there from the police back in Ohio. Hesitating only a moment, she made the call, holding her breath, smoothing her pink blouse and picking off an imaginary piece of lint from her black, striped skirt. On the fourth ring, she was ready to give up when a warm, male voice answered. "Could I speak with Detective Conrad?" She asked sweetly.

"Who's calling?"

"Oh, well my name is Jackie Reed."

"Jackie! This is Detective James Conrad. I'm glad you called me."

"What's going on with Jeremy?" She blurted out.

"Well, I was hoping you could give me some insight about that." James said softly. "Have you thought of something since we last talked?"

"Annie called me and was talking crazy." She said bluntly. "She said Jerr is involved in some kind of killings?"

"Perhaps," James answered. "But, what I want from you is to tell me about the last time you saw him."

"What? That's been so long ago, it's ancient history!" Jackie spluttered. "He was just a teen." Jackie paused and thought a moment. "It didn't start way back then, did it?"

"Do you think it could have?"

"Well, that one little girl died, you know. At a pool party or something. Jeremy was there, but he was only about twelve, or maybe fourteen." A sob caught in her throat. "I mean, well, he was alone with her when she fell into the pool. But, nobody thought he did anything. Like, he was never charged or anything. It was all innocent and he didn't even act the least bit guilty or anything." Another pause. "He didn't do anything then, right?" Came the pleading voice.

"I don't know," James' smooth voice came clearly through the phone. "Truthfully, I haven't looked into that death yet. You're the first one to mention it."

"Well, I won't believe it!" She said with only a slight amount of conviction. "How could you even think that?"

"I, uh, I didn't bring that up. You did."

"Oh, God, am I really thinking that?" She paused again, drumming her long, manicured nails on the table. "Wait! What are you thinking?"

James laughed softly. "I truly just wanted your perspective about the boy so I might be able to measure the man."

"Well, the boy was awesome! He did well in school and was never in any trouble. He loved going fishing and golfing with me. Wouldn't he have shown some signs when he was a boy? I mean, well he didn't talk about his dad, would shy away from the subject, but you know, he saw his dad commit suicide when he was three, or something."

"Yes, I am aware of that fact. And, as far as 'showing some signs,' most people who have a mental illness, a severe mental illness, don't manifest that until they are in their teens or twenties. If that is what we're dealing with now. There are many missing pieces, but thanks for the input."

"Will you keep me informed?" Jackie asked.

"Well, that is more Anna's place than mine. Let's see what happens. It's a long and rather involved investigation. Thanks for your input, though. I appreciate it." With that, he cut off the call and slid his chair over to his computer. "Well, well, well, what can you tell me about a little girl dying when he was a boy?" He pressed keys until he had a screen that showed him the death news about the girl who died at the pool. He whistled, "What a coincidence. She had a bashed in skull from striking her head on the side of the pool… The only witness; Jeremy, of course, said she fell and he couldn't stop her." He sat back in his chair and looked up at the ceiling, clasping his hands behind his head. "What do you know? It's such a classic, it screams to be solved." He turned to look out the large window behind his desk. "Where are you now, Jeremy? What are you doing?"

Jeremy was on his way down another long highway, singing with the radio, enjoying the countryside of southern Illinois. He crossed the mighty Mississippi River, gawking like a tourist. "I never get tired of seeing this big, old river," he muttered. Once in Missouri, he slowed down, looking for a park to camp in for the night. It would be good to sleep out under the stars in his tent. He followed the first sign that pointed to a possible camping area. This was familiar ground. After setting up his camp, he drove toward the Lewis & Clark State Park. He sat in his car on the shoulder of the busy highway, staring at the park sign. It seemed like so long ago he had left Rebecca lying in the park. He was half-tempted to see if the body was still there, to move it, even.

"Don't be stupid, Boy!" Dad yelled at him.

"Shut up," Jeremy growled. He checked traffic as he pulled out into the right lane.

"You're speeding. Slow down!"

"I said for you to shut…up!"

"So, you're gonna sabotage this, after all. That's why you wanted to make this trip. You don't have the balls to…."

"Stop it! Just stop it!" Jeremy yelled. His knuckles were white from gripping the steering wheel in his anger. He pulled off the road and got out of the car, kicking the tire and slamming his fist onto the hood. It left a sizable dent. "Leave…me…alone." He said through gritted teeth. He closed his eyes as he rested his arms above the driver's door. Feeling himself begin to calm, he looked around the area. There were trees and shrubs, some large rocks. He opened the door so he could sit on the seat, his feet on the roadway and his elbows on his knees. "I'm going to do this my way," he said slowly. "I know what I'm doing. Stop hounding my every step. Please!" He looked up at the blue sky pleading, almost allowing himself to cry.

Slowly, he stood up and stretched, arching his back and swinging his arms from side to side before climbing into the driver's seat once again. Back on the road, he made his way to Jamesport in Daviees County. Once there, he trolled back roads, driving slowly past Amish farms and fields. Afternoon turned to evening and the sun was setting when he turned down one more dirt road before heading back to his campsite.

"There she is," Dad whispered.

Jeremy smiled as a girl appeared, walking slowly along the road. It was a wooded area along the road with no houses in immediate sight. "Perfect," Jeremy crooned as he passed the girl and came to a stop.

Thirteen-year old Deborah Bontrager slammed the barn door. One more wrong thing in a day full of them. "Datt (Dad) will start yelling any minute," she predicted, hurrying down the driveway.

"Deborah!" Came the dreaded voice from inside the barn where she had left him. "Deborah!"

"Don't look back. Just keep walking," she murmured, walking swiftly to the road. She turned right on the dirt road, away from other farms, heading toward the woods. There was a trail she often walked that would lead her back to the farm beyond the house. *Datt* (Dad) didn't come after her, but she knew her brother, Jesse, would be along in the buggy soon enough. She sighed. "No privacy; seven brothers and four younger sisters, ugh!" she kicked at a rock and stubbed her bare toe. "Errrrrr!" She moaned, hobbling off the road into the grass towards the woods. She reached a log to sit on, just as a car passed her, pulling ahead to stop. Deborah looked around, wishing Jesse might hurry. Suddenly, her big brother didn't seem like such a bother. She watched as an English man got out of the car, walking slowly toward her. One more look down the road. Nothing. "Should I run?" She whispered to herself as she stood to face the stranger. He was smiling.

"You okay, Girl?" He asked in a gentle voice. "Do you need a ride somewhere, or some kind of help?" He smiled showing his even, white teeth. At least, his lips curled into a smile, but his eyes didn't. He reminded her of a snake ready to strike its prey. She shook her head, "*nee* (no)," she whispered.

"Well, then," he said, running a hand along a metal bar he held. "Run away, Little Girl."

Deborah froze, staring at the man with the smooth voice and dead eyes. "I, my *Datt* (Dad) will be along any minute," she pleaded, hoping it was true.

"Run!" He hissed.

Deborah looked away for one second, her hesitation her undoing, before dropping to the ground. She never knew what happened to her.

In seconds, she was in his trunk, her Kapp resting in the back seat, and he was driving down the road. He smiled at the image of a buggy appearing in his rearview mirror, just before his dust cloud obliterated the view. Jeremy made one stop near a river on a deserted highway. The body slid easily into the water, far from her home. Whistling a tune into the darkness, Jeremy made his way back to the car where he threw the white *Kapp* up front onto the passenger seat before driving to his campsite. Once in the tent, he cut one of the strings from the *Kapp* and stuffed the string into a bag with others. The *Kapp* would go into a box in the car trunk in the morning. For now, he laid it on his pillow, putting a hand on it as he lay down to sleep.

Before dawn fully arrived, Jeremy was on his way to Iowa. "Fast enough for you, Dad?" He sneered into the rearview mirror.

Rhoda Miller woke up before the sun could warm her room. She got dressed in the gray light of early "false dawn" as her father called it. There was much to do on an Amish farm and work started before breakfast. Rhoda was the oldest of ten daughters. "Poor *Datt* (Dad)," she sighed. There were no sons to carry on the family farming business. Rhoda was to be married in a few short weeks and she and her husband would live on her family farm to help her father run his dairy. She smiled as she thought of Gary, her betrothed. He came from a family of eight boys and said he would be glad to leave his childhood home for the farm of her father.

Rhoda made her way down the stairs and past the kitchen where she could hear *Mamm* (Mom) and her sisters preparing the morning meal. Soon, she knew, the house would fill up with the smell of bacon and eggs, pancakes and hot syrup. Her mouth watered at the thought. But, the cows were already beginning to mumble and bawl for their milking. She hurried to the barn to open the door and let the herd into the milking stanchions. The big Holsteins pushed their way past her as each one found their favorite stall. Rhoda closed the metal collars and filled the troughs with silage from the silo at the end of the row of cattle. Helping the goopy mass of feed down the trough with a shovel, she talked and crooned to the impatient cows who were already snapping bites from the feed. She heard the door open and close as her father came in and began the generator for the milking machines. *I'm glad he uses milkers and we don't have to do this by hand,"* she smiled at the thought. Starting at one end while her father began at the other, they methodically wiped down udders and placed the tubes onto each cow. There was no talking. They did their work efficiently, cleaned the equipment and placed the filled milk cans in the cooler for the transport truck, then went inside for their morning meal. "Is this how it will be for Gary and me, never talking, just working and eating, and working some more?" A frown creased her brow at the thought.

"*Dochter* (daughter)," said *Mamm* (Mom)." *Ben je ziek* (Are you ill)?"

"*Nee* (no), *Ik was alleen denken* (I was only thinking)." She hurried on before anyone else could speak. "*Ik ga voor sen wandeling. Doen we iets nodig Yoder's opslaan* (I am going for a walk. Do we need anything from Yoder's store?)."

"*Nee* (no)," *Maam* (Mom) answered. "*Let opde weg* (Be careful on the road)."

"*Ik wil snoep* (I want candy)." Rhoda's three-year old sister said. Everyone at the table laughed.

Rhoda touseled her sister's blond hair. "*Misschien wat snoep* (maybe some candy)," she answered. She soon realized her mistake. All the girls began saying what kinds of candy they wanted her to bring back. Rhoda kissed her mother on the cheek, then walked to her father. He ignored her for a few seconds before turning his cheek for her kiss. "I love you, *Datt* (Dad)," she whispered. She felt his smile as he tried to remain stoic, his lips quivering in his efforts to not show the emotion.

Rhoda walked down the lane and turned right onto the dirt road. Her mother watched her oldest daughter as far as she could see her. It would be the last time she ever saw her daughter alive again.

Jeremy knew it was only a matter of time and patience as he trolled the dirt roads near West Grove, Iowa. He had camped the night before in Green Valley State Park, in a remote corner of the campgrounds. It was a beautiful park, filled with many trails. He was satisfied that he could do what he needed to do and be gone without the slightest trace. "No one even knows what I do," he commented to the air. "Even Mom will be surprised at how I've broadened the scope of what she started."

"Are you just stupid or what?" Dad said from behind him.

Jeremy turned to face him. "What now?" He growled. "I told you I could do this on my own, and I am."

"And when will you finish the job? How long are you going to mess around out here when the target is in Ohio?"

Jeremy shuddered as an image of his mother flitted across his mind's vision. "I'll get to that, but I have a plan. You've seen the map. You know what I think because you aren't even real!" Jeremy's face flamed as he shouted out of control. He punched the back door of his car, leaving another dent. He wiped his face and lowered his head to the roof of the car, close to crying. "Go," he said in a hoarse whisper. "I don't want to see you when I lift my head. Go." Jeremy put his elbows on the car as he held his hands over his face and eyes.

"Look, Jerr," Dad said softly. "I love you. We started this thing together. It was always meant to be simple, you know? It's gotten way too big now."

"Yeah, you, me and Jack, remember?" Jeremy said, lifting his head to stare at the trees across the camp site. A deep frown creased his forehead. "And then that girl got involved. The one from Kentucky. How'd she even figure in to this? You all make me sick!"

"Forget about her," Dad said. "Just focus on the end goal. Let's finish this thing, okay?"

Jeremy shook his head. "Dad, I've set out on this trip and I want to finish it before the end. I know what the end is, but I want to present her with as many hats as she can handle, then it will be over. Get it?"

Dad shook his head, an exact replica of his son just a moment before. "It won't end like you think, Son. You've already set other wheels in motion…"

"Why don't you just shut up and let me live my own life," Jeremy snarled. He jerked open his car door, slid into the driver's seat, and started the engine. His last image in his rearview mirror was a shadowy figure standing in the camp site being sprayed with small pebbles from under his tires. It gave him a small sense of satisfaction.

On a whim, he decided to mail the boxful of *Kapps* to his mother. He drove to a local post office, eyeing the postal supplies. A large white envelope, padded with bubble wrap seemed appropriate. He made his purchase and returned to his car, driving around town until he found a secluded parking area near a Walmart. There, he got the box out of the trunk, neatly folded each *Kapp* and stuffed them all gently into the envelope. He sealed it with tape, he also had bought for the purpose. He addressed the envelope in his neat, concise handwriting, admiring his handiwork. He hefted the package, turning it over and over. It didn't seem to shift, just fluffed out gently with it's precious cargo. Jeremy returned to the post office to mail it.

"Anything liquid, perishable, or glass?" Asked the bored-looking clerk.

"No, it's just…" Jeremy raised his eyes to meet the curious ones of the clerk. He was unnerved, feeling vulnerable suddenly. "It's just cloth," he said quietly, looking back down at the counter. "How much?"

The clerk eyed him once more. "The envelope is a little over-sized," he said. "It'll be $4.79, cash or card?"

Jeremy looked into his wallet. "Uh, it'll have to be Debit," he said, sweat beading up on his face.

"Okay," the clerk was getting impatient with this fellow. "The machine is right there in front of you."

Jeremy swiped his card, completed the transaction, and scurried out of the building.

"Why do you have to act guilty all the time?" Dad yelled at him in the car. "That guy didn't care about you! He just wanted you to mail the stupid package!"

Jeremy held back tears and anger. *Just leave me alone,* he screamed in his own head. *Stop torturing me with all my mistakes! I'll show you! I'll show everybody!* He drove carefully out of the parking lot, turning onto roads that would lead him out into the country.

In under an hour, he found his next target. "This is getting almost too easy," he muttered, reaching for his small bat under the seat. He pulled up ahead of a girl who was wandering slowly along a deserted road, a half mile or so from the last driveway. Little did he know that he was only a few hundred yards from another farm, a busy place where James Yoder had a general store.

Again, the girl (Rhoda) had no idea what hit her. She was wandering along the road and stopped when he got out of his car. At his command to run, she looked confused, just like they all did. At last, she made the right turn and his little bat did the rest. The whir of the bat through the air, the "chunk" as it bit into the soft tissue of the temple, brought Jeremy a feeling of accomplishment, power, control. Another potential woman fell silently to the ground. He scooped her up and put her into his trunk just as a line of three buggies came trotting onto the road from the store. Jeremy was startled at the sudden activity. He wondered what they had seen or heard. He felt as though his limbs had turned to stone and wouldn't carry him to the driver's door of his car. As the first buggy approached, a bearded man leaned out and called to him.

"Got troubles with the car?"

"Wh-What?" Jeremy responded. "Oh," he smiled weakly. "No, no um, just lost." He scratched his head and smiled as convincingly as possible.

"Do ya need help?" The man persisted.

By this time, the other buggies had also stopped. A young man was getting out of the third buggy, walking toward him with a friendly smile.

Jeremy felt his pulse quicken. He could barely think, let alone talk to these men. His right hand lay lightly on the trunk lid.

"*Wie geht's* (How are you)," said the young man, offering his hand.

Jeremy quickly rubbed his hand on his pants and offered his own hand to the strong handshake. He nodded at the man. "I, uh, I'm doing well. I just got lost for a bit."

"Not uncommon out here," the man smiled again. "The highway is only a couple of mile sahead of you. Ya can't miss it." He pointed up the road.

"Yes, well thank you for stopping. Guess I look kind of silly." Jeremy replied.

"Nope, not at all. Have a *gut* (good) day!" He waved as he walked back to his buggy and stepped lightly up into the rig.

Jeremy nodded to each of the buggies as they went on down the road. He blew out the breath he'd been holding and got into his car.

"Too close for comfort. You're getting sloppy," Dad complained from the back seat.

"Shut up," Jeremy growled as he started the engine and drove to the nearest highway. He drove around the countryside, looking for a likely woods or waterway to dispose of his cargo. But, he couldn't find anything suitable. Finally, he drove to his campsite and began a small fire. He sat, slowly feeding sticks into the flames for over an hour, deep in thought and troubled by the thoughts he found in his own mind. Finally, he got up and walked a few of the trails near his camp. He found one he felt he could use. Only a few feet from his car, covered in brush, was a deep ravine. He looked carefully around the camping area. There weren't many campers at this time of year, although a few hardy souls were there. He was fairly isolated from them, but could still see their coming and going. Jeremy opened the trunk of his car and got out his bat. Blood was dried on it, something he almost never allowed to happen. He walked to the small creek and began scrubbing the bat with his handkerchief. To his dismay, the metal was stained and he couldn't get the last of it out. He took it back to his fire and plunged it into the coals. After a few minutes, he pulled it out with a stick to cool. He used some dish soap he carried in his camping kit to wash it off. Now, it was stained and streaked with the scars of fire. Somehow, it made him feel better.

Jeremy didn't sleep. He sat quietly, placing stick after stick into his fire. Finally, in the wee hours of the morning, when he was sure everyone else in the campground was sleeping, he got up and wrapped the body in his blanket, carefully removing the white *Kapp*. He carried her to the ravine and rolled the body to the bottom. "I don't even know your name," he said to the almost invisible form. He slapped his hands together, "Well, good riddance." With that, he loaded up his car and drove away into the night.

As he drove through Iowa toward Illinois, Jeremy was plagued with the faces of so many girls he didn't know yet who had met their ends at his hands. "I didn't know any of their names," he muttered. "Isn't that strange?"

"Why bother with that now?" Dad asked.

"It's like there's a connection, but not," Jeremy tried to explain. "It's just kind of weird."

"So, now, all of a sudden, it worries you?" Scoffed Dad.

"No!" Jeremy said quickly. "Well, maybe it does a little. All I have is a bunch of strings, all alike. It's like the girls never really existed, but I have these strange memories," he paused, "and the dreams." A shudder passed over him.

"Okay, so can we go home and finish this thing?" Dad whined.

"You know, all I heard for weeks was practice, practice, practice. Now it's hurry up and finish, over and over. So, no, we're not ready to go home, as you call it." Jeremy replied calmly as he pulled his car into a gas station. "We're going to wash the car and clean it out, fill it up, get something to eat, and move on." Jeremy drove into the carwash behind the gas station to do just as he'd said. As he vacuumed out the trunk, he noticed a dark stain on the carpeting. "Odd," he muttered running his fingers over the stain. He walked to the passenger side of the car to grab his water bottle. With a corner of his chamois and a little water, he scrubbed at the stain. It became lighter, but didn't go away. "Now, when did this happen?" Jeremy frowned fiercely as he rubbed the stain harder.

"Does this really matter?" Dad asked.

"Shut up!" Jeremy snarled.

"Well really, this is the end anyways, right?"

Jeremy stopped what he was doing and closed the trunk lid. "Is it?" He whispered.

"You know it is. I know it is. Come on, Kid."

Jeremy looked around him as if seeing his surroundings for the first time. There were other people who were nearby, using the vacuums, washing their cars. No one seemed to be paying any attention to him, but he suddenly felt vulnerable, like any one of these people could suddenly begin accusing him. He pictured the woman with the red shorts and white shirt coming up to him, pointing, mocking. He moved to the front of the car, intent on getting out his bat to protect himself.

"What the heck are you doing?" Hissed Dad.

Jeremy looked back, "Didn't you see….?" He paused, darting his eyes at the woman who was busy with her car. His attention was drawn to two men standing close to the building, smoking. They were laughing at something, and Jeremy knew they were laughing at him. He jerked open his door and climbed behind the wheel. Sweat poured into his eyes, stinging. He started to wipe his face with his chamois, then realized what he was doing. Frightened, he flung it to the floor and fumbled for his keys. He was painfully aware that the men and the woman were watching, laughing, pointing at him. He didn't dare look at them. Finally, getting the key into the ignition switch, he started his car and pulled up to the front of the building to get gas. As he pulled up to the pumps, he realized that there were a lot of people. He knew they were all waiting for him to get out. Angrily, he put the car into Drive and sped off. "There are other gas stations," he consoled himself. An hour later, he fueled up at another station, got quickly into his car and drove on. He was almost out of Iowa when he saw a lonely figure walking across a field he was passing. He got off the road at the next exit and made his way back on a road he decided would bring him to the girl, for girl it was, and now she was walking along the road, approaching a small copse of trees. He smiled for the first time this day. "How convenient," he breathed as he pulled into a little-used lane at the edge of the trees. He stepped out of his car and gave a friendly wave. "Hi!" He said.

Barbara looked suspiciously at the stranger near the little car. She looked quickly over her shoulder, but there was no one there. "Hullo," she muttered, head down, as she skittered to the other side of the road.

"Hey, I think I'm lost. Could you help me?" He persisted.

Barbara wanted to run, but didn't know if she should turn back toward work or keep going toward home. Just beyond the trees was a path across her father's hayfield. She could see the break in the fence she often used. Shaking her head at the stranger, she darted past his car to gain her goal. She looked back as he let go of his bat. All she saw was a whir in the air, kind of like a bird coming toward her. She dropped to the ground just beyond his car, without a sound.

"Thank you, Iowa," he smiled. "I thought I was done here," a small chuckle rose to his throat.

"Don't gloat, you Idiot," Dad snarled. "You've got to get out of here. You are taking too many chances."

Jeremy stifled an outright laugh as he opened the trunk and spread out the plastic. He picked up the girl and laid her gently in the trunk, taking time to cut a string from her Kapp before removing it from her and tossing it into the back seat. He went back and shut the trunk, looking around, but there was no one to be seen. He laughed out loud this time, and climbed back into his car, whistling his little tune.

He came to a state park and drove in, paying the day fee. He drove around the park, through the camp grounds and onto each of the narrow roads. At last he found the place he was looking for, near a pond. The roadway ended in a parking lot where two hiking trails converged. Jeremy got out of his car and meandered down first one of the trails and then the other, looking for a depression or ravine suited to his purpose. At dusk, he used his small shovel to scrape a shallow grave into a small, rocky area near a running creek. Being careful not to draw attention to himself, he took the body and placed it gently into the dirt, covering it with the dirt he'd removed and nearby leaves and twigs from the towering trees. Lastly, he rolled rocks over his handiwork. Finally satisfied that the scene looked natural once again, he washed his hands in the flowing water, washed off his shovel and his bat, and walked back to his car.

"What are you digging around for?" Said a park ranger who was parked near his vehicle.

"Uh, nothing, I guess." Thought I saw a dead animal and I was gonna bury it, but I was mistaken." He shrugged nonchalantly.

"Is that right?" Asked the officer. "How far down that trail you talking about?"

Jeremy looked back toward the trail head. "Maybe a half mile, I guess." He shrugged again.

"Are you camped here at the park?"

"No," Jeremy shook his head. "Just here on a day pass," He tried to smile.

"Well then, the gate's gonna close, so you better head on out."

"Yes, Sir," Jeremy smiled as he put his shovel into the trunk and got into the driver's seat. The officer followed him to the front gate and watched as he drove off into the gathering darkness.

Jeremy just kept driving all night. He finally stopped at a small town in Illinois where he paid for a cheap motel room and laid sobbing on the bed. Sleep overtook him, but his dreams were vivid nightmares of dancing Amish Kapps and disembodied eyes tormenting him. When he finally awoke, he was drenched in sweat, twisted up in the blankets, his clothes and shoes still on. He walked out to his car and got his suitcase out of the backseat. Once back inside he stood in a steaming shower, letting the hot water course over his body, hoping it was washing away the dreams and the delusions. Tears coursed down his face, mingling with the running water. "You weren't ever going to cry again, remember?" He spat out at his image in the mirror as he shaved.

After his shower and shave, Jeremy wrapped himself in a towel and laid on the bed in front of the TV. He couldn't find anything interesting, but did finally doze off to the background noise. When he awoke, he felt hungry, so he packed up his few belongings and drove into the rainy day. "I had a plan," he told himself. "I need to stay focused and just finish out my plan."

"Some plan," Dad said from the backseat.

Jeremy frowned at his dad in the rearview mirror. He stopped at a fast food restaurant for a sandwich and kept driving, weaving along on back roads heading mostly north and east. At last, he came to a crossroads on two dirt roads. He sat there contemplating what to do. It suddenly hit him that Dad was right. It was time to go home and finish the plan. "I've wasted so many days and lives," he muttered under his breath. He took out his cell phone and called home.

"Hello?" Came his mother's voice.

"Hi, Mom," Jeremy said in a sad voice.

"Where are you, Jerr?"

"On my way home," he answered tiredly.

"Are, are you okay?" She asked. He could hear a trembling in her voice.

"Yeah, but what's up with you?" A worried frown creased his brow. "Are you crying or something?"

"What? No!" She said too quickly.

Jeremy stared out the window at the muddy road ahead of him. *Something's not right,* he thought. "Is Grandma there?" He asked in what he hoped was a calm voice.

"Yes, she is," Mom almost whispered. "She's been staying here with me for a while now."

"You mean she lives there with you?" He asked, concern causing a wrinkle in his forehead.

Mom laughed nervously. "Well, just about, I guess."

"Why?"

"What?"

"Why? Is something wrong? Are you hurt or something and I didn't know?"

"No, Jerr, no," Mom seemed to stutter. "She just has been keeping me company for awhile and has sort of moved in. I've been lonely, you know?"

There was an awkward silence. "Are you coming home, then?" Mom asked.

"I thought I would, but I don't know. I'm sort of confused, I guess." He rubbed his forehead, the beginning of a migraine causing him pain. "I'm sent you another package," he added. She sighed. He felt it more than hearing it. *She's beginning to know,* he thought in wonder. The silence went on for several seconds. "Okay. Well, I have things to do, but I'll be rolling in there in a couple of weeks or so, I guess."

"That...that long?" She said.

"Yeah," he stated. "I've got some other things to do before I," he paused. "Before I see you again."

"Jeremy," she began. "Please just come home. Let's talk like we used to do, okay?"

"About what?" He was beginning to feel irritated with the conversation.

126

"Just life," she sighed again.

"Mom, Dad and I have plans. I'll be there when I get there. Let's not be in a hurry to end this, okay?"

"What?" Alarm tinged her voice. But, he had hung up the phone.

***

"What have I done?" Anna wailed to her mother who sat with her on the couch, rubbing her back.

"It isn't about you, Dear," she said softly.

"You did just fine," James' deep voice drifted from across the room. "We traced him to a rural area in Illinois. Now that we have his phone on our radar, we'll be following him no matter where he goes."

"He's sent more of those dreadful hats," Anna spat out. "I don't want them! I won't open the package!"

"Shhhh," her mother said. "It's all for the best, Dear. You know it is. He has to be stopped from this awful killing."

Anna looked up. "How can you calmly say something like that?"

"Because it's true."

Anna laid back on the couch and starred across the room at nothing.

"I'll let you know when we have him," James added. "When the package arrives, just give me a call and I'll take care of it, okay?"

"I don't want to know." She shook her head slowly, now staring down at the floor. "How did this happen?" She whispered.

"He's very ill," James said limply.

She looked up. "Yes, like his father." She nodded. "Yes, he is." She looked into the eyes of her mother. "Can we get him help or what?"

"He will get help," James said. "We'll process through the legal stuff, but he will end up in a mental home eventually. I'll keep him from going to jail, if I can."

"How will he live with what he's done?" She whispered again.

"I don't know," he said simply.

"If he's medicated, he could still live a good life," her mother offered.

"Oh, who are you kidding?" Anna said angrily, getting up to look out the window. "He'll never have a normal life or anything like it, medication or not. He's killed over and over. He can't just walk away from that like it never happened."

Her mother sighed. "You're right, of course." She said, tears pouring down her cheeks. "I just want it to be all right for him, you know?"

———

Jeremy looked thoughtfully at his phone. A smile curved his lips as he tossed the phone out into the ditch. "Stupid!" He snarled at himself.

For hours, Jeremy trolled up and down county roads, but to no avail. No one was out on a rainy evening like this. That is, no one was out walking. With a sigh, he turned on his wipers as he found his way out of the county and north toward Wisconsin. Suddenly, out of the murky darkness, his headlights fell upon an older woman walking quickly toward him. He slowed, then brought his car to a stop. She kept coming down the road, walking, no, almost running. He rolled down his window. "Is something wrong?" He yelled.

She stopped in her tracks, doubt filling her features. "*Jah*, (yeah)" she bobbed her head. "An accident up the road a piece. Do you have a phone?" She came toward him.

Jeremy got out of his car and walked toward the trunk. Once there, he hefted the weight of the bat in his hand, preparing to throw it. But, the silly woman kept coming closer, too close. He pointed up the road, "Up there?" He asked.

She looked back into the dark, enough time for him to hit her in the temple with his bat. She yelled out, "Oh!" and fell forward toward his car, hitting her head again on the fender, her knees grinding into the mud. "What?" She looked up at him.

Jeremy didn't know what to do for a moment. This had never happened before. He picked up his bat and hit her again, harder this time. She fell to the mud, her fingers clenching and unclenching into the ooze. Her moaning caused him momentary panic, but as she lay still and became quiet, he pulled her body into the ditch. It was then he realized she didn't have on a *Kapp* at all, just a plain black scarf, and it was matted with her blood. He wiped his bat on the grass as best he could and climbed back into the car. He sped down the road, soon passing a buggy turned over in a ditch, three or four people around it. He kept going. "Drive, just drive," he told himself.

And drive he did, straight to Wisconsin until he came to a 'tourist town' that advertised lodges and motels, restaurants, and a lot of local attractions. He drove around for a half hour, trying to make a decision. At last, he stopped for fuel at a convenience store. He stretched as he got out of the car, realizing that he truly needed to rest and let his body rejuvenate. He used his card, but was suspended in thought as he contemplated how he might be tracked. "I've used it now," he mumbled. "Mom already knows where I am." He frowned heavily as he put the nozzle into his gas tank and set the handle to run. Turning to look around him, he noticed the streak of blood on the side of his car. Panic seized him and rendered him immobile for several seconds. He felt eyes watching him, fingers pointing him out. He was afraid to turn around. His breathing was shallow and his chest began to hurt. Jeremy closed his eyes and waited to hear the sound of the gas pump shutting off. It felt like an eternity. But, it finally clicked off and he moved woodenly to place the nozzle back into the pump. He didn't bother with a receipt, just got into his car and started the engine.

"Well, now aren't you just a mess?" Dad laughed maniacally from the back seat. "Mister, 'I have a plan, leave me alone.' You don't have any idea what you're doing now."

Jeremy starred at his father in the rearview mirror. He couldn't think of anything to say. "What happened to my plans anyway?" He muttered under his breath. "I gotta wash the car right now," he said, looking up at the mirror. He scanned the area for a carwash. There was a sign just down the street. He pulled out onto the street carefully, sure a policeman would be behind him in just a moment.

"If you had a brain, you'd be dangerous," Dad laughed again.

"I don't need this right now," Jeremy growled. He pulled into the car wash and used his card again to wash the car. "She knows," he whispered. "She'll find me here and I'll have to do it here." He shook his head to clear his thoughts. "She must have called the police by now and told them everything."

"Don't act crazy," Dad said. "Just go about your business as usual. "Why'd you come here anyway?" He sighed. "More of your plan, I suppose?"

"I did have a plan," Jeremy was close to tears. "But, she didn't even have a *Kapp*. She messed up the whole thing." He held his head in his hands as his car moved through the washer. "This was never just about killing....it..."

"Isn't it?" Dad was smirking.

"How did this all get started? Why me?" He pounded a fist onto the steering wheel.

"Oh, Poor Baby," Dad mocked. "You know how this all got started. You were chosen to stop her, but you took it all out of proportion. God, what a mess!"

Jeremy sped out of the carwash and into the parking lot of the first motel he found. He backed into the parking spot as usual, removed his keys from the ignition, and turned in his seat to face his father. As usual, Dad could disappear when looked at. He was great at appearing in mirrors. "I want you to go away. Everything's changed now." He grabbed his overnight bag from the backseat and opened his door. His little bat was laying on the seat. "How did that get there?" He muttered. There was blood on it and blood on the seat. He felt the rise of panic again. Quickly, he opened the back door and jammed the bat into his bag. The blood on the seat seemed to scream out at him. He backed up, awkwardly reaching out to close the door. His eyes were glazed with fear and confusion as he stood staring at the stain on the seat. It was getting bigger and bigger as he looked at it, filling the backseat, going to burst through the window at any moment! He wiped at his eyes and shook his head slowly. When he forced himself to look once more at the seat, he realized that the stain was only a little stain after all. "God, I really am losing my mind," he said, wiping first one hand and then the other on his pants. He made his way to the motel desk and checked in. His hand shook as he wrote his name. When the clerk handed him his card, he stared hard at it, hesitated to touch it. As he felt the clerk staring at him, he finally picked it up and slid it into his wallet. He glanced up at the clerk, smiled weakly, and followed the proffered directions to his room. It was on the third floor, directly above the parking lot. He looked out the window at his car. There she was, standing beside the car, looking straight up at his room. Her green dress was dripping with blood, and she held the black scarf in her hand. It was trailing on the ground. He looked at the front bumper of the car and saw the blood streak in the place where he had just washed it. Jeremy fell backward, catching himself with the edge of an overstuffed chair. He sat quickly, sweat pouring down his face. "It can't be real," he said, staring at nothing. "It's impossible." With a moan, he moved over to the bed and curled up in the coverlet where he slept the day away. He awoke sometime in the night, lights from the parking lot flooding his room. He closed his eyes and rolled over, but it was no use for now he was awake. Slowly, Jeremy made his way to the bathroom and closed the door. He used the facilities and turned on the shower. Hesitating, he wondered if he really needed to take off his clothes. *Maybe I should just wash them and my body. Maybe...* he shook off the thoughts and walked into the bedroom. Without looking out the window, he closed the drapes, lifting his bag onto the bed and dumping the contents, using just the light coming out of the bathroom. He pulled out clean, if wrinkled, clothes to wear, just a tee shirt and boxers. "I'm not going anywhere," he mumbled. As he stepped toward the bathroom, there was a knock on his door. Jeremy stared at the door with fear. *Who knows I'm here?* He thought. There was another knock, so he slowly crept to the door, peering out the peephole. A waiter of some kind stood outside in the hallway. "Who is it?" Jeremy said too loudly.

"Um, room service, Sir," came the muffled reply.

"What do you want?"

"I have your dinner order, Sir."

"What are you talking about?" Jeremy opened the door to see a young man with a covered tray on his arm. They locked eyes for a few seconds.

"You ordered the steak dinner. Here it is." The lad held up the tray with a crooked smile, trying not to stare.

"I didn't order anything," Jeremy answered. "What kind of trick is this? Who sent you here?" Jeremy poked his head out the door and looked up and down the hallway.

The waiter took a step back, worried that he had made some kind of mistake. He looked at the ticket on the tray, then at the door. "One steak dinner with a side salad for this room," he stated matter-of-factly. "It was called down about, let's see, two hours ago; to be delivered at seven pm."

"I was sleeping," Jeremy ran a nervous hand through his hair. "I don't remember ordering this." He looked toward the bed where a hotel menu lay next to his blanket. With a slight shake of his head, he motioned for the waiter to bring in the meal. "Over there on the table," he pointed toward the corner of the room.

The waiter turned on the overhead light, approached the table, and laid out the meal and opened one of the two bottles of beer. He turned to look at Jeremy. "Anything else?"

"No," Jeremy said sheepishly. *I must look like a fool.* Quickly he reached for his wallet and gave the waiter $5.00. "Thanks," he mumbled, holding open the door.

"Thank you, Sir," smiled the waiter as he went out into the hallway. Jeremy let the door close, locking it for the night. He walked over to the table and looked at the food. It was a great looking meal, but he didn't think he could eat. He became aware of the sound of water running and looking around, saw steam coming from the bathroom. He rushed into the room and turned off the water, then turned it back on and undressed, stepping into the hot water and enveloping steam. "None of this has happened," he crooned to himself, letting the water run over his body. "It was all a nightmare. I'll walk out there and everything will be normal." He dried off, got dressed in his under ware and stepped back into the bedroom. His eyes were drawn to the table and the meal placed there. Automatically, he walked to the table and sat down. The food was cool, but still edible. Jeremy choked down some steak and rice, but couldn't eat. He never touched the beer. "I've never ordered anything so foolish in my life," he said into the room.

He got out one of his water bottles and downed it, tossing the empty bottle toward the trash can, but missing it by far. He laid on his bed and was soon snoring loudly in the empty room.

A subtle sound woke him before daylight. Someone had slipped a paper under the door to the room; the bill, most likely. Jeremy rubbed his eyes then pushed his fingers through his hair. He surveyed the room, realizing that he had slept with the lights on, including the light in the bathroom. He let out a long sigh, placing his hands under his head. "What's wrong with you?" His voice sounded loud in the early morning stillness. There was no bustle yet from other motel patrons rising that he could hear.

"I'll tell you what's wrong," said Dad from the other side of the room.

Jeremy looked balefully in his direction. "Pray, tell me all my failings," he said dryly.

"You don't follow orders and you got yourself into a pickle. You left a dead body out there for everyone to find."

Jeremy yawned. "In Iowa or someplace, right?" He muttered.

"Yeah, so why aren't we in Ohio already?"

Jeremy smiled to himself. "Cause I'm doing things my way. Should I break out into song?" He laughed at his little pun.

"Seriously, Jerr, you're in trouble here."

"Oh, so now it's all my troubles, huh?" Jeremy half sat up to look at his father, sitting at the table. "You had nothing to do with any of this!"

"You know what?" Dad said quietly. "No. No, I didn't have anything to do with any of it. This has been all you, this quest for bonnets and strings. This was never the plan at all. And, even if I did have something to do with it, I'm dead, right? Who's gonna listen to a dead man?"

Jeremy threw a pillow which hit the table, knocking over dishes and bottles. "So what!" He yelled. "I never planned any of this either, you know! It was her, all her!"

"Okay, then why this ridiculous quest? Let's just go home and call it quits."

Jeremy rolled over and hid his head under the remaining pillow. "Leave me alone," he growled into the blankets.

After a few minutes, Jeremy sat up and then walked into the bathroom. When he came out again, the room was empty. He strode to the window to look down at his car. It was sitting there in the daylight of early morning. No one was near it. He felt relief and a great sadness. He couldn't explain it, but it was there. "I'll just go home," he muttered. "There's nothing left of my plan really. I don't feel like I need to do it all now. Maybe Dad was right, I should have just finished up his plan a long time ago." He threw his things back into his overnight bag, took one more look around the room and let himself out quietly. There weren't many people in the hallways or dining room. He grabbed a bagel and headed for his car after settling his bill. As he passed out through the glass doors, he spied an ATM machine in the corner. He went to it and drew out as much cash as was allowed. Then he went to his car in the parking lot. He inspected the car, all the way around. There were no telltale signs, no blood anywhere. *I really am losing it,* he thought as he threw his belongings into the backseat.

By habit, Jeremy drove out of town and found back roads that would take him south, and out of Wisconsin. He whistled a little toon, trying to find a radio station to listen to. At a little diner, somewhere in the countryside, he watched an Amish girl and her friends laughing and talking near some buggies tied to a hitching rail. Finally, they began to disperse, climbing into the rigs and driving away. All except one girl. She might have been twelve or twenty, it was hard to tell. He watched her pick up a backpack, sling it onto her back, and walk around the building. "Probably got a pony cart or something back there," he mumbled. He reached for his overnight bag and drew out his bat. He rubbed it lovingly before laying it on the passenger seat of his car. To his surprise, the girl reappeared, riding a bicycle out to a side road in the opposite direction from the way the buggies went. He hefted his bat once again. "One more?" He whispered with a slight smile. He watched as the girl became smaller and smaller, then disappeared over a hill. There didn't look to be any trees down this road, but no visible houses either. The houses seemed to be back long lanes from the roadway. Jeremy caught one more glimpse of the girl as she went over another hill, then she was lost completely from his view. Whistling his tune, he drove slowly down the dirt road. There were no power poles, just open fields. In between two hills, he found his quarry, wading in a small creek. "What is it about wading barefoot in a creek?" He mumbled to himself. He pulled his car off to the side of the road, cracked his knuckles over the steering wheel, and climbed out, his bat stuffed securely in his pants pocket.

"That water must be cold," he observed to the startled girl.

She looked up and down the road before returning his stare. A timid smile played around her mouth. "Not so bad," she murmured lowering her eyes. She looked through her lashes at her shoes and stockings laying on a rock a few feet from her. "I...I better go now," she said as she sidled away from him and grabbed her belongings.

If she hadn't looked back, if she hadn't taken that one last glance at the stranger, she might have made it to the brambles near the ditch. But, she did what he knew she would do, that glance over her shoulder. The bat embedded into her temple and she dropped into the water. Jeremy nonchalantly removed her *Kapp* and washed off his bat in the rushing water. "One more, Mama," he said as he threw the *Kapp* onto the backseat.

He left the body lying in the creek, her golden hair flowing on top of the water.

Once in his car, he wasted no time getting himself onto a major highway out of the state. He drove through the night, crossing through Illinois and into Indiana. He stopped at a truck stop for a shower and quick meal, wondering when it was he had last eaten. Carefully, he paid for everything with cash.

The Talk

Detective James Conrad was frustrated because they lost the phone signal. There was no telling where Jeremy had gone, what he might be doing. He put out feelers to all law enforcement in a seven-state grid. He was looking for killings that could fit the MO Jeremy had set, looking for the little tan-colored Kia with Pennsylvania license plates. After a few days, he was rewarded for his patience with reports of an older woman and a 15-year old girl in Iowa and Wisconsin, respectively. He carefully placed pins on the map to represent the latest kills, as he waited to receive paperwork to confirm the deaths and circumstances. "Where to now, Boy?" He asked the leader board.

"You have a call, Sir," Darren, another detective informed him.

James walked to his desk and pushed paperwork aside so he could answer the phone.

"Anything new?" Anna's plaintive voice asked.

He sighed. "No, Anna. I don't know where he is yet. I'd hoped this was a call from someone with more information. Unfortunately, it would be because there have been more, uh, well…."

"More killings," she whispered, close to tears.

"Yes," he sat heavily in his chair.

"All right, then." She said.

"Did you get any new packages?"

"Not since the one he told me about, the one I gave to you," she sniffled into the phone. "Mom thinks that means he's stopped."

"What do you think?"

"I think he's just saving them up. Probably doesn't want to spend the money on postage."

I'll tell you what," he said. "I'll pick up you and your mom around six tonight and we'll go out to eat somewhere. We can talk about our theories, if you want. Maybe, just maybe, I'll have some new news by then. Yes?"

"I don't know," she hesitated. He could hear her talking to her mother. "Mom says it sounds like an excellent idea," she laughed. "So, I guess we'll see you around six. Actually, do you just want us to meet you somewhere so you don't have to come clear out here?"

"No, that's all right. I don't mind coming out there. Besides, all the really good restaurants are out that way."

"Okay," she hung up the phone.

About an hour later, James did get new information. Darren brought him the news. "Two more," he said. "This time from Illinois, again. Our boy's on the move."

There was no doubt; two girls within twenty miles of one another, each with one lethal head injury, their bodies left in a ditch or along a creek bed. "What is it about creeks and Amish girls that draws his attention?" James mumbled at the map on his wall. "At least now he isn't burying them or dumping them in some park or other."

"I think it's just opportunistic," Darren said. "I think he trolls country roads until he spots one of these girls walking somewhere and strikes them down. They often go barefoot, so that isn't odd. Maybe they wade in the creeks along the road on their way home, too. They might look for rocks or shells, you know? They're a simple folk."

James smiled. "And our boy has had plenty of experience with the Amish. They do seem to be his principle target."

"Agreed. The girl in Kentucky was just another opportunity that fell into his lap, so to speak."

James nodded.

"So, from previous patterns, where to now, do you think?"

"Indiana, I suppose," James frowned. "But, what's the ultimate goal?" He studied the map again as he had over and over during the past weeks. "What is he doing? There has to be a goal. I don't believe it's all totally random."

"At first, you thought it was about his mother. Have you considered he's making his way to her?"

"Yeah, that is what I think. But, he also told Anna that he's on his way home. That could mean Pennsylvania."

"Lots of Amish between where he is now and Pennsylvania," his co-worker observed.

"What do we know about his life out there?" James turned his attention to a large file. "Hmmm, not extremely well-liked, kind of reclusive, but nobody seems to have hated him. He didn't make enemies, just didn't make friends." He thumbed through papers, then turned to the computer. "Very successful at property sales, though, until he seems to have quit." He compared kill dates to work dates. "Yeah, he couldn't concentrate on them both. He quit working to pursue his delusions." James dialed the number for a local psychologist he knew. "Hey, Doc," he said into the phone. "I've got a case I'd like you to review. Tell me what's making this boy tick, and what his next move is gonna be." Pause. "Yeah, I know you can't make predictions, but just tell me what you think, okay?" Another pause. "I'm sending it to you right now. Let me know as soon as you can, okay?" He listened for a few seconds before hanging up the phone. Just before he was ready to leave for the day, he received the answering call.

"Interesting case," the doctor stated. "It isn't about the hats or the girls, but almost assuredly about his mother. Most likely dealing with Schizophrenia or Schizoaffective Disorder. His father was diagnosed with it. That's not a diagnosis, by the way."

"That's what I figured, too," James replied. "Can you tell me anything new?"

"Right now, I'd say he's practicing so he can make the final kill. Are you prepared for that?"

"Yeah, we're waiting for him to show up."

"Does she understand?"

"I think so, but she's not ready to admit it. I'm seeing her and her mother tonight. It's part of the conversation I plan to have with them both."

"He's very ill."

"Would medication help?"

"Maybe. There's a lot that has to happen before we could even get him on medication. His mom won't be the last kill, you know."

"Yeah, I do know. I hope we can prevent all of it when he does make his move here."

"Where is he?"

"Illinois or Indiana, I suspect. He got rid of his phone and made a large withdrawal from his bank, so I guess he's paying cash wherever he is. Unfortunately, bodies are the only trail we have right now."

"Wow! I'd really like to talk to him. From what you sent me, he's like a boy in a man's body, living out his delusions, absorbed by them. From the notes, I'd say he has hallucinations of his father, and is believing he's doing what the father wants. Let me know when you have him in custody."

"Sure thing," they rung off. James took one last look around the office, grabbed his keys from the desk, and headed out the door. He arrived at Anna's house shortly before six pm.

They were ready, coming out the door as he pulled into the driveway. Anna waved as he emerged from the car and opened car doors. "I'll sit in back," she said as she lithely slid into the backseat.

"Oh, for heaven's sake!" Jean commented, going around the blue SUV to the passenger side.

James laughed at them both as he sat behind the wheel. "Where to, Ladies?" He asked.

"What about Justin's?" Anna asked. "It's kind of private and we have a lot to talk about, don't we?" She smiled sadly at James in the rearview mirror.

"Justin's, it is," he nodded as he backed down the driveway.

It was a country restaurant, very popular with the locals. There were booths and tables, but the best feature were the secluded booths in the back. They made their way to the one in the farthest corner, away from all the other patrons. They ordered their meals, then sat back to wait, an awkward silence settling over them. The waiter brought them drinks, then they all went to the salad bar. Once seated, James began to talk.

"I got some new information from Illinois," he hesitated, taking a bite of salad.

"More?" Jean asked, her face turning pale. Anna moved the food around her plate with a fork.

James nodded. "Yes, I'm afraid so." He glanced at Anna, worried that she looked not only drained of color, but like she wasn't sleeping, and wasn't eating.

"When will he stop?" Anna choked out, not looking up.

James reached for her hand which he covered with his own. "I don't know, but hopefully soon."

"Please take at least one bite, Dear," Jean said to her daughter. "You being sick isn't going to help anything."

Anna flashed her mother a look of anger, removing her hand from James' grasp. She wiped her mouth with her napkin and folded it neatly, laying it on the table. "My son is out there killing innocent girls, and you two," she looked from Jean to James," you two, want me to eat and act like life is just going along like usual!" Tears flowed down her face. "I'm sick of all of it! I'm half sick of you!" She looked pointedly at her mother.

James placed his hand on her shoulder. "I can't even begin to imagine what you're going through, Anna," he said softly. "I'm sorry if I came across as crass or uncaring. I care very much."

She looked at him and saw the sincerity of his words. *I wish,* she thought, then shook her head slowly. *What a stupid thing to think! Here I am worried about Jerr and thinking thoughts about some man that surely cannot ever come true. How stupid of me!* She slumped a little and looked down at her plate. "Sorry, I just don't know what to think, let alone what to say. Just ignore me and say what you need to tell us." She mouthed a 'sorry' at her mother before she picked up her fork again, but only pushed at her salad.

The waiter interrupted with their main course before they could talk again.

"Where is he going now, or do you know?" Jean asked.

James shook his head. "No clear idea about his short-term goal, but I believe we know what the ultimate one is."

The two women looked up, all attention on his handsome face. Jean looked suddenly at Anna, then back at James with a question in her eyes. He nodded at her, his mouth set in a grim line. "Oh," she breathed.

Anna stared back down at her food. "He's going to kill me last of all, isn't he?" She asked, her voice barely above a whisper.

"No," he said sadly, holding her hand again.

I wish he wouldn't do that, she thought as her eyes traced how their fingers seemed to fit together. It suddenly dawned on her what he had said. "Really?" She asked, looking into his eyes to see the lie.

"Really," he said flatly, looking right at her.

She squeezed his hand. "Are you sure? I thought we'd decided a long time ago that I am a target, maybe THE target for him."

James smiled. This was the first animation he'd seen in her for a while. *She is a beautiful woman,* he thought. He moved to take her hand in both of his, supper completely forgotten. "You are a target, Anna," he said softly. "But…" he put one hand up to touch her mouth as she began to protest. "You are not the final goal."

She closed her eyes and withdrew her hands to cover her own eyes. "I see," she said, trying not to fall sobbing into his arms. "I see."

Jean watched the whole interaction in amazement. Even though they were here under such awful circumstances, she could clearly see the attraction between her daughter and this man. *A healthy relationship with a normal person,* she thought. *Oh, don't be wretched! Anna loved Charlie and he loved her the best he could. No one knew until after the wedding that he had such awful problems. He tried, though; he really tried. And he gave us Jeremy.* "So, he inherited his father's illness," she stated causing the other two to acknowledge her presence. She looked from one to the other. "Yes, I'm still in the room," she smiled.

Anna blushed, but James simply smiled back. "So you are," he said, picking up his fork and taking a bite of his cooling food. He winked at Anna causing her to blush again.

"Mother," Anna said quietly, but with a small smile of her own.

"Does he need to die the same way?" Jean asked.

"We're doing everything we can to intercept him either at his home or at yours, Anna," he smiled at her.

"I've noticed all the attention from police on our street," she said.

"Why don't you just stay at the house with us, James?" Jean asked, trying to look innocent.

"Mother!"

"Well, why not?" She asked. "That's what they do in the movies."

James laughed out loud. It was music to Anna's ears and she looked at him with open admiration. *How long since you heard a man laugh spontaneously,* she thought.

"I could, you know," James said, a slight tease in his voice.

"That's not necessary," Anna said. *I wish you would, though,* she thought. Her eyes betrayed her thoughts to him. She sighed. "Our main goal should be to keep Jeremy safe," she said. "He mustn't be hurt, although I don't know how to do that." She looked pleadingly at James. "He's not only ill, he's very dangerous, isn't he?"

"That's true," he answered. "This is serious."

"What would the future hold for him?" She thought aloud.

James sighed, rubbing his eyes with the tips of his fingers. "If his mental condition can be documented and determined a factor in his case, he could be placed in a long-term, probably life-long residential facility, not prison."

"We could visit him there," Jean said hopefully.

Anna choked on a small bite she had taken. "Mother, it would be a life he'd never grow accustomed to. I certainly wouldn't want to live like that. He's intelligent and strong. It would kill him."

James sighed again. "The only other option is prison," he muttered, half under his breath.

They finished their meals, what they could eat of them and James drove them home. Anna sat in the front passenger seat at her mother's insistence. "I'll arrange for an officer to stay at the house," James said. "Jeremy is headed this way and we don't know exactly where he'll turn up."

"Oh, no…" Anna started to protest. She sighed again. It was becoming a habit. "Yes, I see that it might be for the best," she said sadly.

"If he contacts you, let me know right away. Try to find out where he is and when he plans to come here, if you can."

"Yes, I will." She said with a sad smile. She put her hand on his and squeezed. "Thank you, James. I mean it."

"I'll at least talk to you every day," he said. "It will be all right. We'll stop him and it will be all right somehow."

"No, it won't," she said. "It won't ever be all right again. But, it will be over and he can get the help he needs, I hope." Tears welled in her eyes, then spilled down her cheeks. She didn't wipe them away. "I hope he doesn't have to die for it to end."

James reached up and wiped her tears with his thumbs. "Me too," he said before he kissed her lightly. He looked into her eyes. "Me, too."

Endings

Jeremy just kept driving. He felt nothing, noticed nothing along his drive. In northwest Indiana, he spotted a sign that indicated a road to Michigan and took it. He drove through the countryside, turning wherever he felt he wanted to turn. It didn't matter to him anymore...

Enid

Enid Schwartz had been babysitting for her sister-in-law all day. She was tired and angry because she had to walk home. *Datt* (Dad) *could have come to get me,* she thought now. She kicked at a pebble along the road and stubbed her toe. "Ow!" she screeched, more angry than need be. She hopped on one foot for a while, then plodded along again.

"Exercise will do you good," Esther had told her when she complained about having to walk once again.

"I know everyone thinks I'm overweight," she moaned.

"Well, you are," Esther had said unkindly.

Now, Enid just wanted to get home as fast as possible so she could doctor her stinging toe. It was only a mile away, but seemed like ten. She saw a car up at the stop sign. It wasn't an odd thing, but this one had a Pennsylvania plate on it. She veered off to the left side of the road near a small copse of trees, ready to make her turn at the corner. She didn't see him, just heard a strange kind of whirring sound before feeling a blast to her head. She fell to the ground silently. Her *Kapp* came off and a swift hand caught hold of it before the wind got to whisk it away. He pushed her

144

into the ditch, noting her heaviness. "Too much chicken," she murmured. He smudged the tracks of his boots from the dirt road, got into his car and drove away.

Jeremy continued to drive. He felt like his mind was on autopilot. He stopped somewhere and put gas in the car, went through a carwash, and drove around on backroads. He wasn't sure where he was, but it didn't matter. He wasn't sure when he had eaten last. That didn't matter, either. He didn't feel hungry or thirsty, just driven to go....*where are you going? I don't know and I don't care,* his thoughts confused him. He couldn't be sure if he was talking to himself or if Dad, or maybe even Jack, were talking to him in his head. "They're both dead, you know," he muttered. "Well, maybe not Jack, but she definitely killed Dad. You saw it; you know what she did, how she started this whole thing." *They'll be looking for you. They know by now and they'll be watching.* He shrugged. "Does it matter? It's almost over anyway."

He crossed the state line into Indiana sometime in the night. On a secluded road, he slept in his car. In the early morning, he simply waited along a dirt road and soon enough there she was, a female walking along the road by herself. "Stupid Girl," he muttered. The bat hit her in the face, going through the eye socket and into her brain. She lay twitching on the ground. It took some strength to extract the bat it was embedded so far. And she wouldn't hold still, kept moaning, too, clawing at him. Jeremy finally got his bat and wiped it clean on the bottom of her brown dress. He grabbed the *Kapp* and threw it all into his trunk this time. She was already in the ditch, alongside a rusted fence. "Stupid, stupid Girl," he said again before driving off.

Carl Stolfus watched in horror as his cousin was murdered. He'd been bringing the horses up for a day of work when he'd noticed the brown car near the woodlot. There was a man standing in the trees, looking at the road. Carl assumed the Englisher was relieving himself there in the woods.

He noticed Karen, his sixteen-year old cousin walking along the ditch on the opposite side of the road. He was about to wave at her when he heard an odd whirring sound and down she went. He stood beside one of the large work horses, holding tight to its mane. He was afraid to move, afraid he would be next to die. He was sure she was dead. There was blood all over, the metal rod sticking straight out of her eye. The Englisher bent over her and pulled the rod out. It took him some time to get it, then he wiped it on her choring dress like it was a rag, or something. Carl felt like throwing up, but he daresn't move. He leaned into the broad shoulder of the mare and prayed. When the car finally left, Carl waited for a few minutes to be sure the man wasn't coming back. He walked to his cousin and picked her up, carrying her to her home a quarter of a mile back down the road. He relayed his story to the shocked and grief-stricken family, then they all waited for the police to come. One of the boys had gone to make the call. The police took their statements and looked at Karen's body. Carl felt embarrassed at the attention, and that strangers were looking so intently at his cousin. They wanted to take pictures, but thankfully, Uncle John wouldn't allow it.

Carl had to take the investigators to the scene where she had died. Her blood was still on the ground. Carl wanted to kick dirt over it and cover it up. Finally, the ordeal was over. He was allowed to go home to his own family. He noted as he walked along the road that his brothers had pitched in and gotten the horses working the fields. He felt guilty that he'd not been there to help. "I'll never go English, that's for sure and for certain," he said as he walked along. "Theirs is a crazy world."

Jeremy drove on, taking the toll road into Ohio, then turning off into the countryside, winding his way down to Holmes County. He avoided the area where he knew his mother lived. "I'll be there soon enough," he said out the open window. The breeze felt good on his hair. He ran a hand into the unruly locks, noting how long his hair was getting, and the feeling of it being greasy. He looked into the rearview mirror. "How did I let myself go like this?" He wondered aloud, rubbing a hand over the growth of stubble on his chin.

He pulled into the parking lot of a small, out of the way motel with cheap rates. They were happy with his cash payment. The room was dingy, but clean. He took a shower, taking time to trim his hair and shave. "I'll bet I haven't shaved in a week," he said amazed. He scrutinized himself in the mirror before flopping on the bed where he was soon snoring in sleep. At last, he awoke, looking around the room furtively. He took another shower before dressing for the day and driving off into the countryside.

Nothing looked promising, but it truly didn't matter. He headed generally east toward Pennsylvania and his home. *Not too smart,* came the thought. It was just a thought, not a voice. *Where's Dad?* Jeremy wondered idly. "Well, that doesn't matter, either," he said into the afternoon sun. He felt heavy, like his arms and legs weighed 'a ton.'

He came upon the girl and her broken bicycle quite by accident. There she was, on the side of the road, grease all over her hands....

Patty rode her bike to the store for her mother nearly every day, it seemed. There was always something the large family needed. She was twelve and felt useful when she could go to the store to get things for *Ma'm* (Mom). "*Wie geht's?*" (How are you?) she asked the woman behind the counter at the country store.

"*Gut, gut,*" (good, good) was the reply.

Patty walked around the store gathering the few things her mother had sent her for. She stopped to pet the dog and admire the puppies in her pen with her. "Are you selling the *hundlin* (puppies) yet?"

"*Ja* (yes)," she answered.

"I'll tell *Datt* (Dad), he's always looking for a *gut hund* (good dog)." Patty paid for her purchases with coins that were wrapped carefully in her handkerchief. "*Denki* (Thanks)," she said sweetly before leaving.

On the way back home, Patty decided to ride off the road on a small trail she and her brothers often used. It was fun to ride over the little hills and jump over tree roots and around rocks. However, as she came around the big rock near the roadway, she skidded and fell, her chain coming off the sprocket. Patty got right to work fixing it, getting grease all over her hands and dress. "*Mamm will let ungerennt,* (Mom will be upset)" she said as she tried to wipe the grease off her hands and onto grass. She became aware of a car coming slowly down the road. She watched him drive by, then set up her bike and pedaled quickly down the road. She had to pass him because he stopped just ahead of her.

He waved at her. "I'm lost," he explained.

Patty hesitated. She knew she shouldn't speak to strangers, especially Englishers. It would only bring trouble. She stopped her bike to look back. The man standing beside his car was the last vision she ever had.

Patty was found late in the afternoon in a small ravine near the copse of trees by the road. Her bicycle was lying beside her, and her *Kapp* missing, revealing a single wound to her temple, blood matted in her hair. It worried her mother that she had been exposed so, her hair down and splayed out on the ground.

At last, Jeremy neared his home. Pennsylvania seemed much like every other state he'd travelled through. He didn't feel a sense of relief like he thought he would. As he approached the lane that led to his home, he noticed a utility truck parked on the county road. There were no workmen, just the truck sitting there. Something about it made him feel uneasy. He drove past his road and kept going to the small town about twelve miles east. Once there, he gassed up his car and bought some snack foods and water. He watched carefully out the windows for unusual activity, especially police vehicles. The town seemed as quiet as usual, but something was up. The clerk in the convenience store seemed nervous, over-talkative and friendly. Jeremy paid for his purchases in cash and walked with seeming calm to his waiting car. He drove east out of town and turned north toward the interstate. "There's no use in going home," he said aloud. "I might just as well get this whole thing over with."

"Finally using your brains, eh?" Dad said.

Jeremy ignored him. He watched for a county road to turn onto. *I'll show the old man,* he thought. *He'll learn sooner or later who's in charge of this now.* Jeremy glanced into the mirror, but Dad was nowhere to be seen. "Chicken," he said to the mirror.

He trolled road after road, turning right and left through the countryside, travelling in a mostly northwest direction. He saw lots of families, farmers and their sons working the fields, even girls and their mothers working gardens and yards, but no one was out walking the roads.

"Maybe they know," Dad said. "You've been pretty stupid over the past few weeks. You've left a trail that a blind man could follow."

Jeremy glanced at the rearview mirror once again. Dad stared him straight in the eyes. "I don't need you, you know," he said quietly. His voice was menacing.

"Yeah, Big Man, I know. You've got it all figured out." Dad laughed before disappearing once again.

Jeremy slammed his palm on the steering wheel. "Run away, why don't you? It's what you're good at! You've always taken the easy way out!" Jeremy was suddenly assailed by memories, picture after picture of life when he was a child. He was powerless to stop the scenes playing through his head. He saw his mother and father fighting over a large knife. But, Dad was too strong. He slid the knife from Mom's grasp and cut his throat, showering them both with his blood before falling to the kitchen floor. Jeremy cried, having to pull over on the side of a road to sob over the scene he just witnessed. "Mom didn't do it," he croaked into the still air. "No, I know what I saw!" He screamed out, wiping the tears from his face and rubbing his hands on his pants. "She never even cried! She never held onto me. She just went on like nothing ever happened." His tears were spent and he felt exhausted. "Like she didn't care..." he finished slowly. Jeremy got out of his car and walked around it twice, thinking about what he had just seen as though it was the first time he'd ever seen it before. "That's not what happened," he whispered. "I know what happened, don't I?" Sweat poured down his face and back. He placed his palms on the hood of his car and let the sweat drip off his face. "I don't know what to do," he said quietly. "What have I done?" A shudder shook his body. He slowly looked up, trying to get his bearings. To his right was a field full of cows. To his left, a woods with a farmhouse behind it. There was no one in sight. A mosquito buzzed his ear and he absently slapped at it. He leaned against the hood of the car, crossing his ankles, his arms crossed. "I can't even call her," he muttered, as fresh tears threatened to fall.

"Blah, blah, blah," Dad said from beside him. "Now you're gonna feel sorry for her and for yourself, and the whole deal is off."

"I'm not listening to you," Jeremy replied.

"You haven't been listening to me for a long time, Boy."

"This has all been wrong. I've….I've…" He couldn't speak any more, just vomited right there in the road. "Get away from me," he croaked when he finished coughing. He got a water bottle from the car and took a long drink after spitting out the first swallow.

Something happened then that he wasn't expecting. As he looked up the roadway again, he saw a young woman walking toward him. In her hands she carried the carcasses of two dead chickens. He watched them sway with every step she made, their scrawny necks swinging in an eerie kind of rhythm. It reminded him of the day he watched his friend's mother killing chickens. His sight filled with a red haze as he felt bile rise up into his throat once again. He grabbed his gloves and his bat from inside the car. As she got closer, he bent down and picked up a rock which he threw in her direction, but off to the left. As he suspected, she turned to watch where the rock went, a frown of worry creasing her brow. When she turned back to face him, his bat found it's mark through her left eye. She let out one cry, dropping slowly to the ground, moaning and writhing in pain. "Not again," he whispered, watching her grotesque movements. He suddenly realized that she was pregnant, very pregnant. *Two for one,* he thought. *But, what if that child's a boy?* He shook his head to clear the disturbing thoughts. After a moment, he started toward her to retrieve his bat and her *Kapp,* but heard the distinctive clip-clop of horse's hooves coming down the road from behind him. "It's done," he announced as he got into his car and sped away, leaving the telltale evidence on the road.

Coming Home

Jeremy drove through the night toward Cleveland. It was time to finish what he'd started. "I'm finished," he said aloud in the comfort of his car. "That back there, was the end for me."

"What about our deal?" Dad asked.

Jeremy drove in silence for several miles. "I should never have listened to you," he finally stated. "I should have told Mom about you and put you away in your grave where you belong." *What will become of me?* He thought. *Prison, a hospital, locked up for life?*

"You know better than that," Dad said. He sat in the passenger seat. "We'll finish it and you will come to be with me... forever."

"Was that the plan?"

"You know it is the plan."

"A knife again, I suppose? Since that's your specialty."

"Don't sneer at me, Boy. This was always the plan, and you know it."

Jeremy turned up the radio, drowning out any further conversation. He drove into the night, ever coming closer to home. *Huh...home,* he shook his head at the thought.

Nearing the city where he grew up, Jeremy pulled into the cemetery, driving to the grave of his father. "You stay here," he said to the empty seat beside him. "There's no need for you to be there." He left his car near the gate, in a small parking lot. Stretching as he got out of the car, he breathed deeply several times, shoved his hands into the pockets of his light jacket, and began the walk to his mother's street. In his pocket was a string; the first string, the one with the stain on it. He fingered it over and over. It was eerily comforting.

James Conrad and Anna sat in her living room, enjoying a cup of tea together. Jean was tending a fire in the fireplace, not for heat, just for the coziness. "So, he was right here in Ohio," Anna breathed.

James nodded. "As of two days ago, yes."

Jean turned, a poker in her hand. "Why can't someone stop him? We know what he drives, after all."

"What we don't know is where he is driving it," James replied softly. He reached for Anna's hand. "I'll stay here now until he comes."

Anna nodded silently, sipping from her cup.

Jean frowned. "I thought you were going to stop him when he went to his own house. Must we go through him coming here?"

"Jean, if I could be certain he will go there, I would wait there." He looked at Anna. "But, Anna is my priority. He's going to end it all here."

"When did he start hating me?" Anna asked plaintively.

"He doesn't hate you, he loves you; but, he does hate what he believes you did." James said softly.

"Why didn't we know? At the beginning, I mean, why didn't we know?"

"Would you have believed it?"

Jean sat down in the overstuffed chair across the coffee table from the couple. "No, she wouldn't have believed it. She didn't believe it for a long time."

"True," Anna nodded. "I find it hard even now."

"So, do I," Jean agreed with a sigh. "It's like a bad TV show, but we can't turn it off."

James' phone rang and he answered it. Little was said on his end, but he was listening intently to his colleague telling him about the latest victim, in Pennsylvania. "Thanks," he put his phone on the coffee table.

Anna closed her eyes, "More?" She queried.

"Yes,:" he nodded, "near his home in Pennsylvania. He drove past his home, never stopping there. Now, he's on his way here."

"Are they following him?" Jean asked.

James shook his head. "No. No, this time he left his bat and didn't take the *Kapp*. I'm taking that as a sign that he's done, that something has happened this time causing him to panic."

"Like what?" Jean asked. "He goes around killing innocent girls and now he panics over this one?"

James looked directly at Jean, shaking his head, his eyes pleading for her to drop the conversation. "I can't be sure," he mumbled.

Anna looked from one to the other of them. "You're keeping something from me," she said. "Please don't ever lie to me, James, or keep secrets. Please don't do that."

He nodded, blowing out his breath before speaking. "This time," he said, "this time, he was seen by someone, the victim herself. She isn't dead, but has a severe brain injury. She's pregnant, and they will birth the baby yet tonight. Her brother and his girlfriend were in a buggy, coming down the road and saw him get into his car and drive away, leaving the woman on the road."

Oh, my," Jean breathed.

Anna cried openly, laying her head against James' shoulder. He held her lightly while she cried out her misery.

They all heard the screen door squeak at the same time. "That's the back door," Anna whispered, squeezing James' hand hard, raising her head to look toward the kitchen.

"Let me get it," he said calmly. "Call Darren. He'll know what to do." He rose from the sofa and walked into the entryway that would lead him to the back of the house.

Jeremy was startled by the strange man who walked into his mother's kitchen. For a moment he thought he must be in the wrong house. As he looked around in confusion, he realized that everything was familiar; everything except this stranger. "Who are you?" He frowned.

"Hello, Jeremy," the man offered him a hand. "My name's James Conrad."

Jeremy starred at the hand then looked up into the man's face. His eyes were dead serious. "Where's my mother?" Jeremy asked, not shaking hands with James. Instinctively, he knew this man was a policeman of some kind.

"She's in the living room with your grandmother," James replied calmly. "Why don't you and I have a talk before you see her?"

"Are you a counselor or a cop?"

"Does it really matter?"

Jeremy looked away. Everything was the same, the dishes, the table and chairs… "I just want to talk to her." He half-whispered. "I need to tell her…I, uh, need to tell her…"

"What is it?" James asked softly.

Jeremy started to go around the island, but James blocked him. "Talk to me first, Jeremy," he challenged.

"No," Jeremy shook his head. "No, it has to be her." He looked longingly toward the living room. "Mom!" He yelled. "Mom, are you in there?"

"I know the things you've done, Jeremy," James said. "That's why I can't let you see her right now." He paused. "I need to know she's safe."

"From me?" Jeremy scoffed. "Who are you, her boyfriend? I'll bet you're not even a cop, are you?" Jeremy began to pace in front of the sink and stove. "She's not even here, is she?" He challenged. "You better watch out, she has a habit of getting rid of men she lives with!"

"And what do you do, Jeremy? Kill innocent girls and women?" Anna appeared in the dining room doorway.

Jeremy stopped pacing as he watched James move between them. He wanted to laugh. But, he suddenly wanted to cry as grandma walked into the room, placing her hands on Anna's shoulders. *All they can see is a killer,* he thought. *They don't understand why, that there even is a why.* He closed his eyes for a moment.

James' phone rang, breaking the moment. "I need to answer this, Jeremy. It's important that I do." He drew it from Anna's hand. "Yes!" He barked into the phone. "Yes, Jeremy's here with us. Don't come in yet. We're all right." He hung up and turned to Jeremy. "Isn't that right? We're all okay, here."

Jeremy walked to the table and sat down, his head in his hands, elbows on the hard surface. "I know you didn't do it," he whimpered, looking furtively at his mother. "And now, well," he splayed his hands on the table. "And now, I have…" His eyes looked vacant, like he was no longer inhabiting his body. He put his head down on the table, choking on a sob.

Anna made a step to run to him, but James held her back, slowly moving his head back and forth. Her mother held tighter to her shoulders. "He's my son!" Anna breathed.

"I know," James answered.

Jeremy looked up. The scene sickened him. "Now you cry," he hissed at his mother. "All those years you never cried when Dad died, but now you cry." He could hear Dad cheering him on, feel his anger rising. The red mist began to cloud his vision. He was vaguely aware of several other people walking up behind them. He stood up and walked to the cabinet where he knew there would be a knife. *Guess it'll be your way, Dad,* he thought with a slight smile. He knew he didn't need to talk to Dad, just think about the conversation. That was comforting. Talking seemed like a great burden.

James watched the man, Jeremy, walk to the cabinet near the stove. He opened it, revealing cups. *"He's getting a drink?"* James thought. But, Jeremy pulled out a butcher knife and held it to his throat.

"Oh my God, no!" Anna screamed.

"Don't do it, Jeremy!" James said firmly. "We can talk this out. There are other answers to this problem."

"Really?" Jeremy asked, sarcasm replete in his voice. "Prison? A mental hospital? Isn't that what they do with someone like me?" There was no emotion in his voice now, only the words, sounding hollow and sad.

"I love you, Jeremy," Anna said, pleading with her voice and eyes.

But, Jeremy was beyond listening. Red mist filled his vision, clouding all he could see. He looked at all the people in the house standing just a few feet from him. *It's like being on stage,* he said to his father, glancing to his right where he saw him standing near beside him. "I thought I told you to stay away," He said quietly to Dad

"Thought you needed some help to do this," Dad answered with a smile.

"Who's he talking to?" Jean whispered.

"Charlie," Anna and James answered together.

Jeremy looked back at the group in front of him. "Good bye, Grandma," he said. "I'm sorry your daughter started this," he explained, drawing back the knife as though he would throw it at his mother.

That's all it took. The room came alive with gunfire as several trained officers prevented Jeremy from throwing a weapon at one more person. He dropped silently to the floor in a growing pool of his own blood.

"No-o-o-o-o!" Anna yelled as she ran to him, cradling his head to her heart. This time, no one tried to stop her.

"Was that what he wanted?" Jean asked. "Was he really going to kill her?"

"I believe he had clarity and wanted this to end, so he took the avenue that seemed like it would do what he needed. I'm so sorry." James held Jean as she cried.

"So am I," she said through her tears. "So am I."

Oh, Jeremy," Anna said to the still form. "Why?"

He gathered a breath. "I know now what Dad felt that last day," he said, coughing slightly. Pain etched his face, a gray pallor tinging his skin. "It's okay, Mom." He moaned in pain. "I misunderstood and Dad kept telling me what to do. It's finally over… Believe me, it's better this way…." He shuddered with his last breath.

In the days following the private funeral, Anna and her mother wrote cards of apology to every family of the girls Jeremy had killed. They sent the cards with the *Kapps* and the single strings they found in a drawer in Jeremy's house, when they cleaned it out. To her horror, Anna found that Jeremy had kept detailed notes in journals about where each *Kapp* had come from, at least the state, sometimes a detailed description of what he'd done or some landmark he had admired wherever he was, and she was able to send them all away. She explained about his mental illness, but not about what started him on his macabre journey. She sold both her house and Jeremy's, moving in with her mother, using the money to support an Amish school she found in a newspaper ad.

A year later, she and James married. He took a new position in Idaho and they moved there to begin their new life. Jean, of course, went with them. The only momento Anna kept was a picture of Jeremy when he was nine years old, and another one of him graduating from college. His smile belied the tormented mind, gave an image only of the beautiful part of his life. "There is beauty in imperfection," she reminded herself.

THE END

Printed in the United States
by Baker & Taylor Publisher Services